BEAUTIFULLY
BROKEN

BEAUTIFULLY BROKEN

From the Horizon Home Series

Samantha Baily

ELM HILL

A Division of
HarperCollins Christian Publishing

www.elmhillbooks.com

Beautifully Broken
From the Horizon Home Series

Published in Nashville, Tennessee, by Elm Hill, an imprint of Thomas Nelson. Elm Hill and Thomas Nelson are registered trademarks of HarperCollins Christian Publishing, Inc.

Elm Hill titles may be purchased in bulk for educational, business, fund-raising, or sales promotional use. For information, please e-mail SpecialMarkets@ThomasNelson.com.

Publisher's Note: This novel is a work of fiction. Names, characters, places, and incidents are either products of the author's imagination or used fictitiously. All characters are fictional, and any similarity to people living or dead is purely coincidental.

Library of Congress Cataloging-in-Publication Data

Library Congress Control Number: 2019932357

ISBN 978-1-400324880 (Paperback)
ISBN 978-1-400324903 (eBook)

CHAPTER ONE

My name is Etta Alby. I was born in Rancho, California in 1879. The United States had recently declared slavery illegal, and California was a state at the time—part of the United States of America.

My story is confusing and sad—with hardships and suffering. It is a story of resilience and self-discovery. But my story is what shaped *me*.

My mother died from birthing me, and my father died sometime while she was pregnant. I never knew either of them—so I cannot say I miss them—but I do wish I had gotten to meet my parents at least once or twice—so I would have memories to cherish. After my parents passed, I was immediately sent to live with my great-aunt Gertrude Badger, who raised me. Her attempts to transform me into a proper lady failed—much to my relief and downfall—for she put me to work instead of sending me to school when I was ten years old. I did most things her servants performed—laundry, dishes, scrubbing the floors.

There was one thing I loved, however: The horses.

Aunt Gertrude's stepbrother constantly brought her horses as gifts, and she either sold them or used them for her carriage. I mucked their stalls and turned them out to pasture—and escaped to be in their presence whenever I could. Aunt Gertrude despised animals, but took pride in having valuable carriage horses to escort her to her fancy parties.

She considered me a ragamuffin, not fit to be seen in public. So, when I was ten years old, she made a decision: I would never leave her house to go anywhere. Luckily, Aunt Gertrude's stepbrother, John, came to see me every two months or so. He brought me small gifts each time—most of which Aunt Gertrude confiscated—but I found joy and comfort in John's mere presence, anyway.

We went for walks, and he taught me many things about the horses. He would ramble on about 1849, a year when gold was plentiful in California and many were rushing from far and wide to retrieve it. I was so fascinated by all his stories—his knowledge—that I began to dream of living somewhere far away and going on adventures.

John and the horses were my only passages of escape from Aunt Gertrude until I turned eleven, and I met Bonny.

I was scooping manure quietly when loud, anguished neighs filled my aunt's stables. Two grooms clutched ropes that connected to the halter of a beautiful draft mare with a flow-ing blond mane and tail. Her ears were pinned flat against her skull, and she reared, the silky hairs around her ankles swirling. The muscles rippling across her shoulders and chest proved her to be a match for the two men, who she practically swept off their feet as they struggled to drag her into a stall.

I stood rigid for a few precious seconds—staring—then I rushed forward, crooning to the mare. The grooms observed in open-mouthed wonder as she lowered her fore-hooves to the wood floor with a loud SLAM! and extended her muzzle toward me, nostrils flaring. Her ears slowly moved forward. I rubbed the pink snip between her nostrils and grabbed hold of her halter, pulling her head down so she couldn't rear. Her dark eyes met mine.

"You know," a deep voice boomed, startling the mare so that she jerked the halter from my hands. "My father always said that in every handful of people, there's at least one who's a horse wizard. Do you have the gift?"

I curtsied to John, Aunt Gertrude's stepbrother. With his graying hair and easy smile, I wished *he* could have adopted me. He reached over to take the mare's lead-ropes from the grooms. To my surprise, he handed them to *me*!

I studied the mare. Her mane fell to her sleek shoulders—as long and unkempt as my wild, curly, reddish-brown hair. Her coat was grey-white, and her muzzle black except for that pink snip. She bent her slightly-dished face down to me.

"She's the most beautiful creature I've ever seen, sir," I decided.

"Then keep her," John replied, and burst into laughter at my aghast expression.

"Aunt Gertrude will never permit me!" I protested.

"I'll take care of that old grouch," John chuckled, and patted my shoulder. "Take your new horse into her new stall and give her a good grooming. I've never seen her answer so well to anyone. She's definitely yours, Miss Etta."

I beamed and worried at the same time, leading "my" horse into her stall so I could groom her. She bobbed her head and slammed the door with her chest until I stroked her neck to calm her.

"You're so pretty, I'll name you Bonita," I crooned. "But I'm going to call you Bonny. That was my mother's name."

Bonny sighed and lowered her forehead

5

to my chest. I brushed her coat clean, combed her mane and tail, and picked the dirt from her enormous hooves.

John soon returned to the stables and observed me. "Your aunt and I made a deal," he said. "You can keep the mare as long as *you* do all the chores for her: feeding her, grooming her, cleaning out her stall, and exercising her— along with your regular chores. I guess this means you're going to have to learn to ride?"

I beamed up at him.

He taught me to ride Bonny, with a saddle as well as bareback. I even learned to file her hooves with a rasp so they'd stay in good shape.

Early each morning, I mucked Bonny's stall and turned her out to pasture. When my other chores were finally complete, I groomed and rode her.

When I was 13, I taught Bonny how to obey my commands without a saddle or bridle—in case something ever happened.

When my left heel pressed to her barrel, she turned right; when my right heel pressed her barrel, she turned left. If I leaned back and squeezed her shoulders with my knees, she halted. When I tapped my heels to the fronts of her shoulders, she backed up. At first, we both confused and irritated one another. Gradually, and with practice, we learned to cooperate.

John thought it amazing.

"Etta Alby, you are a horse *wizard*!" he told me gleefully. "I want to see you use your gift with other horses someday."

I only smiled at him.

I turned fifteen in 1894, and Bonny turned nine years old. We were both outgoing and inseparable. One day, Aunt Gertrude walked into my bedroom while I busied myself scrubbing the baseboards. I curtsied to her, but she ignored me.

"My stepbrother John died yesterday," she announced, her face expressionless. "I just received word of it. He grew very sick."

"I'm terribly sorry, ma'am," I murmured quietly. I had loved John. Who besides the horses would be kind to me now?

"Don't be," Aunt Gertrude laughed

bitterly. "He was an eccentric old man, and he poured newfangled notions into your head." She dropped a small bag into my hands. "He left this for you. Did he leave anything for me? Of course not—but I'll soon make up for that."

I looked up at her.

"Four years ago," she continued. "John and I made a deal that you could keep that crazy horse as long as you performed all the necessary tasks for it. Now that he is deceased, that bargain is complete. I'm selling that beast."

"What?!" I cried out in horror. "You *can't* sell Bonny! She rightfully belongs to me!"

"Which is about to change—mark my words!" Aunt Gertrude snapped. "It is out of my good heart, mind you, that I'm allowing you to keep whatever is in that bag. Don't try my patience. You are an uneducated ragamuffin who has already proved that you are no lady. Do not even attempt to have a logical argument with me!"

Without another word, I stormed past her and out to the pasture where Bonny grazed. She lifted her head and whinnied at my approach. I climbed the fence and onto her broad back. We rode out the gate and toward the fields.

Rancho was brown and dry, but the big blue sky stretched farther than the rolling hills—out yonder to the mountains. Bonny broke into a gallop while I cried into her silky mane.

"The old witch wants to sell you!" I sobbed. "John is dead, and you're my best friend—you're all I have left."

She slowed to a steady canter and flicked an ear in my direction.

"I won't let it happen," I muttered, wiping my eyes. "I won't lose you."

We turned and galloped back to the pasture. Tonight, I would take Bonny and leave. Maybe we'd find a town with a blacksmith who needed an apprentice. I already knew how to file hooves—how much harder could shoeing be? Or perhaps I'd work my "magic" (as John called it) on horses other than Bonny.

Whichever one I chose, I only wished to escape Aunt Gertrude, to live for myself, and keep my horse. I gave Bonny a thorough rubdown and deliberately left her in the pasture.

She swivelled her ears in confusion, but grazed nonchalantly.

I wrapped my arms around her strong neck. "Tonight, we'll leave, girl."

Bonny nickered softly and nuzzled me. I kissed her pink snip and headed for the house. Aunt Gertrude met me at the door.

"Where have you been?" she thundered.

"I—I…" I stuttered.

"Go to your room!" Aunt Gertrude shrieked. "I don't want to see you until morning!"

I glared hard at her and stomped into my room. Tears that threatened to spill were diminished by anger. Looking down, I noticed the unopened bag from John. I bent down to pick it up. Scooting to the edge of my bed, I opened the bag and rummaged through it. There was a leather hackamore, which I assumed to be for Bonny. I traced a finger over the ornate designs decorating it. The bag also contained a small but sharp knife, a set of saddlebags, and a small pistol.

I gasped when my fingers found a silver chained pendant with a note attached. I studied the little pendant—a round circle with the black silhouette of a horse's bowed head and neck. I unfolded the note. It read:

Dear Miss Etta,

This pendant belonged to your mother, Bonnie Alby. The pistol was your father's. I am gifting the knife, saddlebags, and hackamore to you because I wish for you to have them. Open the left saddlebag, and you will find money. I only wish I could live long enough to tell you more, dear little Etta. You are a young woman now—too old to remain in Gertrude's coldhearted care. I want to tell you of an opportunity: Out in the desert, a little more than 4 days' worth of travel from where you live, silver has been found. It was found 13 years ago, but people from far and wide are still flocking to the new mining town— men and women with dreams in their heads. 'Calico', they call this mining town. These people have horses, don-keys, and mules that will need their feet taken care of. There may also be obstinate animals that need you to work your magic on them. Go to Calico. Chase your dreams. Follow your heart. I believe that God would want me to tell you to be so rebellious. You must stay true to yourself, Etta, and be strong and brave. Good luck, and may God be with you.

Sincerely,
John

P.S. One last thing, my dear: The Romans used to say to their soldiers: "Fortune favors the brave, the bold." My father always said, "Fate loves the fearless." I believe you to be fearless, Etta. The future has a deep attraction for those who have no desire to escape danger. Fate loves the fearless.

Tears of realization rolled down my cheeks. I quickly smeared them on the sleeve of my dress.

"I'll go to Calico, John," I whispered. "Bonny and I will call it home. I'll be fearless."

There was thirty-dollars in the left saddle-bag. I fastened the pendant around my neck, slipped the knife into my dress pocket, and secured my father's pistol and John's note in the right saddlebag. I packed my few neces-sary clothes into a bundle, and added a favorite book to the saddlebags.

All my life, I'd longed for a place to *really* call home. Living with Aunt Gertrude hadn't satisfied my longing. Would Calico be home?

I waited patiently for Aunt Gertrude to blow out the gas lamps at 7:30, as usual. At 8:45, I crept into the kitchen in my tattered gingham dress and sturdy work boots. I shoved apples, bread, and a canteen of water into my saddlebag, and snuck into the stables.

The horses pricked their ears and shifted restlessly at my approach. Praying that they'd remain silent, I packed grain for Bonny into my saddlebags, grabbed her rug and saddle, and started to creep outside, when footsteps sounded. I frantically ducked into the tack room, heart pounding. One of the grooms was making his last nightly patrol, whistling softly. I held my breath. His footsteps faded, and the light of his candle diminished.

Light! That reminded me that I should have matches. I groped the tack room shelf until I found a box of matches. I felt guilty stealing, but Aunt Gertrude owed it to me. She'd bullied, starved me, and just been plain cruel many a time. I marched to the pasture with my shoulders squared beneath the weight of my luggage.

Bonny greeted me with a shrill nicker. I shushed her and placed the rug and saddle upon her back. She stood still while I tightened the cinch, strapped my luggage to the saddle, and slipped on the hackamore. I checked my saddlebags one last time to make sure I'd remembered to pack the rasp for filing hooves. According to John, this tool could change my life.

I opened the pasture gate, led Bonny out, and swung into the saddle. I kissed my mother's pendant, mustered up my courage, and patted Bonny's neck.

"Here we go, girl," I whispered. "To Calico."

CHAPTER TWO

Bonny and I set off at a canter. I wasn't exactly sure how to get to Calico—but if we followed the Butterfield Mail Route, I knew it led to Oak Grove Stage Stop. I could risk asking for directions there. That could start us off proper. My stomach rumbled from no dinner, but I ignored it. Food would be scarce on this journey—so I might as well get used to feeling hungry.

The cool summer night wind whipped my unruly hair into my face, despite my efforts to tie it back. This same wind would follow me to Calico. I kicked Bonny into a risky gallop—in case someone discovered we were gone. Her mane streamed into my face and warmed my hands. I mostly let her choose our route—I just wanted to get as far away from Aunt Gertrude's house as possible. Soon, Bonny began to sweat, and I steadied her into a lope.

"Sorry, girl!" I apologized.

She only snorted in response, probably thoroughly enjoying her new freedom. She and I both knew that I couldn't really control her—she chose to obey me out of love and devotion. The moon glimmered and the stars glittered overhead, so I took it as a sign of hope and good fortune.

Bonny veered into a cluster of trees, farther from civilization. I tugged at the reins, and she settled into a smooth, swift trot. To ease my pounding heart, I tried singing a tune John had taught me.

Oh California, yes that's the place for me
I'm bound for San Francisco with
my washbowl on my knee!

"John said that that's a tune the miners sang when they came to find gold from our state," I chattered to Bonny. "In 1849, a man named Jim Marshall found gold at Sutter's mill. People were coming from all over, hoping to get rich. That's why folks are moving to Calico—they're hoping to get rich on silver. You and I are just trying to find a home. Would you like to hear another song John taught me?"

She grunted in reply, so I sang:

Oh Susanna, no don't you cry for me
I'm off to California with my tin
pan on my knee!

I sang both verses a few more times before cooling Bonny down at a walk. "Let's stop and rest now, girl."

I dismounted and tied her to a tree root sticking up out of the ground. She gazed at me expectantly when I plopped to the ground to spread out my bedroll.

"Sorry Bonny, you have to keep your saddle on," I smiled guiltily. "If something were to happen, we want to be prepared. There might be robbers around here."

Bonny nipped my arm rather sharply and bent her head to graze. I lay down and was fast asleep before I knew it.

Bonny nudged me awake approximately three hours later. It was now pitch black, with no moonlight to guide me. I lit a match and used it to see as I packed up my bedroll, untied Bonny, and mounted. John had always said that horses were able to see better in the dark than humans, and that was why he never used blinkers on his equines.

I trusted Bonny to walk us further toward the next town, following the winding dirt road. I sang the first tunes that popped into my mind for the next hour and a half. Then we stopped to rest again. I removed Bonny's saddle, rubbed her down, and cinched it back on again. She swished her tail in frustration, but didn't nip me. I curled up on my bedroll and slept until early morning.

No robbers bothered me that night.

In the morning, I ate an apple and a slice

of bread while Bonny grazed. She stamped her hoof and nipped at her saddle, desiring to roll, but we couldn't risk that.

"No, girl," I said firmly. "Aunt Gertrude will be searching for us by now. We need to hurry to Oak Grove Stage Stop and get directions to Calico."

I heaved myself into the saddle and clapped my heels to my mare's sides. She bucked half-heartedly and broke into a gallop. I cooled her down just before the Oak Grove Stage Stop came into view. Then I wrapped an old shawl around my head and shoulders to hide my hair. It would look odd in summer, but my hair would surely give me away if Aunt Gertrude was to send someone after me.

The tumbledown station building looked to be abandoned. I spotted a friendly-looking old man sitting on the porch, smoking a pipe. Cautiously, I dismounted Bonny and approached him, tugging my shawl tighter.

"Pardon, sir?"

The old man jerked his head to look at me full. "Yes? May I help you?"

"Well, this is the Oak Grove Stage Stop…" I glanced back at where Bonny stood waiting, untied. "I need directions—I'm off to visit family," I lied.

The old man smiled. "You've got right intentions, but this stage station hasn't been in operation since 1861." He took his pipe out of his mouth as I stared at the ground, embarrassed. "Anyhow, I can give you directions. You'll be needing a map. Where're you off to?"

"Calico—the mining town."

"Calico? All by yourself? Gee, you must be a daring one."

"My uncle will meet me halfway," I lied again, feeling guilty. "But I really do need directions."

He nodded and pulled a pencil and piece of paper from his pocket. "I'll draw you a map."

"Will you draw it showing me how to get *all* the way to Calico—in case my uncle isn't able to meet me? Just in case?"

"Of course, young lady."

For a few minutes he scribbled on the sheet of paper, drawing and labeling. "You'll be traveling a good 150 miles, with or without your uncle. Is that mare tough?" He pointed to Bonny.

Pleased to finally be noticed, my mare plodded up and slung her head over my shoulder.

Thank you God, for such a loyal horse.

"She's tough," I said confidently.

Bonny nibbled at my fingers as I rubbed her muzzle with the tips of them.

"That's good," the old man mused. Then he raised an eyebrow. "It's summertime. Hotter n' hell."

"Yes…"

"You've got no hat. Do you think that shawl will keep your skin from burning?"

I looked shamefully down at my threadbare dress. "I can't afford a hat, sir."

"Well, I can." He took off his own hat and plunked it onto my head, over my shawl.

The sudden movement caused Bonny to eye him suspiciously.

I removed the hat from my head and examined it. It was dusty white, with a crooked rim and a worn leather band, but it was lovely.

"Thank you, sir. Thank you so much. God be with you."

The old man laughed and shifted his pipe to the opposite side of his mouth. "God be with you, young lady—and your beautiful mare. The two of you are going to need Him more than I do."

CHAPTER THREE

D espite the heat, Bonny was impatient to
get moving that day. She worked herself
into a sweat, and I forced her to stop and rest
while I took a few sips from my water canteen.
We traveled at least twenty miles that day. Part
of the time, I walked beside my horse to calm
her and give her a break from my weight. She
hardly noticed.

That night, I dared to remove her saddle.
Bonny rolled, flinging her hooves in the air and
grunting with pleasure. Then she bucked several times before accepting the grain I offered
her. My own food supply was growing low, no
matter how I rationed it.

"We'll buy more food the next chance we get," I told Bonny.

She shook her mane and cropped the grass. I re-saddled her sometime during the night. The next morning, we set off again. We made two rest stops, and I practiced shooting at targets such as specific leaves or twigs with my father's pistol, promising myself I'd buy more bullets when I bought food.

Later that evening, we reached San Bernardino. I desperately hoped that the old man's map was correct—and that we were in the right place. When we came across a general store, I hitched Bonny to a post and went inside. I purchased food for myself and for Bonny, and bullets for my pistol. I was counting my change beside Bonny when a little boy scurried over and snatched the coins from me.

"Hey!" I yelled. "Give those back!"

But he was already gone.

"Did Jimmy take your money, miss?" a voice inquired.

I looked down to see an eleven year old boy with glasses, freckles, and floppy brown hair, in a newsboy cap. He grinned sympathetically at me.

"Yes—is Jimmy that boy's name?" I wondered.

"Yep, that'd be Jimmy!" the young boy replied. He stuck out a hand for me to shake. "I'm Albert Redfield. Everyone calls me Bert. Who're you?"

"I'm…" I paused. I needed to be careful with whom I shared my name. "I'm Elizabeth Badger. Nice to meet you, Bert."

Bert grinned wider, pulling his cap down lower on his forehead. "Nice to meet you too, Miss Badger. I'm real sorry Jimmy stole your money. He's an orphan, you see. It's the only way he knows."

Sympathy welled in my heart. "Tell Jimmy that as long as he puts that money to a good cause—and uses it to feed himself—it's all his."

"I will," Bert agreed. "Gee, that's some horse you got there!"

Bonny tossed her forelock proudly when he patted her shoulder.

I smiled. "Thank you, Bert. Now, I should really get going. I have a long way to travel."

"Where're you headed?" Bert questioned.

"Off to meet an uncle of mine, so he can take me to visit family." I adopted my old lie. "It was nice meeting you, and I wish you well."

"Same to you!" Bert called as I mounted Bonny and started to ride away.

What an agreeable young man!

Bonny and I trekked far that day. I repeated the process of leaving her untacked for part of the night. It was hot the third night, and gnats flitted among the trees. I waved my hat constantly at them, and Bonny's whiplash tail never ceased snapping back and forth.

By daylight, I practically fell asleep against my horse. She butted my chest with her forehead until I tightened her cinch and mounted.

California was much more beautiful and vast than I'd ever imagined. The desert was colorful, the sky deep and blue, and the smell of sage comforting. My heart soared at the sight of it all. I belonged to myself now—and I could explore it all.

"We belong to ourselves now," I told Bonny cheerfully. "We're nearing the Cajon Pass, pretty girl. The Mojave river starts there, and we can practically follow it to Calico. Are you up for that?"

Bonny shook her mane.

"Don't be silly—you want to get away from Aunt Gertrude as much as I do! Don't you?"

Bonny flung her chin up, then down, and I smiled. "I knew it was true." I paused, wondering how silly folks might think I was if they knew I talked to my horse more than I did to people. I shoved the thoughts out of my mind. Besides God, Bonny was my dearest friend.

The Mojave river ran near the top of the Cajon Pass. A flood of relief washed over me at the sight of it. I decided to settle down for a nap.

I stopped to nap in the shade of some trees at one point. One minute I was dozing, the next Bonny's whinnies filled my ears. I jumped to my feet.

A young man, about two years older than I, stood with his horse and pack mule. He was tall and lanky, with scraggly black hair. In one hand he held Bonny's reins, and she pawed the earth mistrustfully.

"Your horse ran off, and I found her at my camp," the adolescent boy said with a frown. "You didn't tie her."

I swallowed. I must have forgotten to tie up Bonny in my hurry to grab some extra sleep.

"Thank you for retrieving her," I replied.

The boy raised an eyebrow. "You're alone."

"Yes."

"You're a *girl*."

"*Yes*."

"Be careful."

"Thank you kindly."

"I'm Timere Westcott."

"I'm Elizabeth Badger."

I thought I saw him grin slightly at my words, but I brushed it off. He handed me Bonny's reins.

"Where are you headed?"

"To meet an uncle."

Timere frowned. "You and I both know

29

that's a lie. If you're going to lie, you need to look at a person full—not at the ground. Where are you *truly* headed? I mean no harm."

"To Calico," I confessed. "I should be on my way."

Timere nodded. "God be with you. Goodbye, Miss *Badger*."

I shot him a suspicious look, but he was already leading his horse and mule out of sight. I took a swig of water and mounted Bonny. She tugged at the reins, eager to move.

"You really shouldn't have run off like that," I reprimanded her as we trotted. "He could have stolen you! I guess it's my fault for not tying you up, though."

Hoofbeats sounded behind us.

Timere was back.

His piebald gelding matched paces with Bonny.

"I was just thinking…" he began. "I'm headed to Calico, as well. What if we journeyed together? It's dangerous for someone to be alone out here."

I glanced at him suspiciously. "You hardly know me, Mr. Westcott."

"Maybe I'd know you better if you told the truth, Miss *Badger*."

I threw up my hands in defeat. "You ought to work for a sheriff, questioning suspects."

"Care to tell me your real name?"

I fingered my mother's pendant. "I'm Etta Alby," I said quietly. "But I can't go by that name until I'm sure I'm safe."

Timere asked no further personal questions. "So, would you care to journey together?"

"Can you be trusted?"

"I believe I can be. Can you?"

"Yes."

"Then let's go."

I warily agreed.

Timere suddenly halted his gelding. "Hey, you know what?"

"What?"

"I like 'Etta Alby' much better than 'Elizabeth Badger'."

I couldn't help but smile. "Me too."

CHAPTER FOUR

The horses slowed to a walk. I studied my new companion's gelding—a slender cart horse with a thick white mane and tail, bushy brown forelock, and blue eyes.

"What is your horse's name?" I asked.

"Elm," Timere answered. "And Grouch is the mule. I'm going to sell him soon. I'm running low on food."

"Me too."

We rode in silence for a while at a trot again. I wondered if I could really trust Timere. I realized I had no choice *but* to. There were robbers that would take more than my left-over change. I needed extra protection in case

I weren't able to reach my pistol or escape in time. I heeled Bonny into a soothing canter, and Timere allowed Elm to follow. When I felt the urge to sing to my mare, I reminded myself I wasn't alone.

A red-tailed hawk screeched and circled overhead. Sagebrush swayed in the breeze. A gopher ducked into its hole. The world was alive and at peace despite the brutal summer heat. I steadied Bonny to an easy jog.

"What if you sold Grouch to a rancher… or a miner in Calico?" I suggested to Timere.

He pulled up Elm. "I'm not sure."

"You could trade him for a dog."

"I don't need another mouth to feed."

I frowned at his hard-set jaw. "What's the matter?"

"They wouldn't trade or buy from an 'injun'," Timere said bitterly.

I stared blankly at him. "Lots of people buy and trade Native American goods."

He halted Elm sharply. "Do I look like an Indian to you? Be honest."

I studied him carefully. He *did* look very

33

much Native American, with his high-set cheekbones and broad shoulders, but his shoulder-length hair was slightly wavy. "Mostly."

"I'm only half," Timere informed me. "I got all the looks of my father. If only my skin weren't so bronze I might be able to pass for a white man."

"It's not something to be ashamed of," I assured him. "It's not *better* to be 'white' or worse to be 'bronze'. God makes us the way He wants us."

Timere looked angry. He nudged Elm into a trot. The gelding surprised me with his gentle patience—especially when Grouch, supposedly true to his name, flapped his big ears and nipped at the gelding's hindquarter.

Bonny tried to gallop twice, begging for her head. She arched her neck and brought her nose to her chest, somewhere between a trot and a canter. Her mane cascaded from one side of her crest to the other.

Timere and Elm flew past us with Grouch at their heels. I noticed that the mule was no

longer connected to the gelding, yet he still followed faithfully.

"Give her her head," Timere called. "I'll
race you to those bushes!" He pointed to a
clump of sagebrush.

I laughed and loosened the reins. Bonny
surged forth with speed that defied her pow-
erful bulk. With determined strides she evaded
Elm. The gelding champed his teeth and soon
matched paces with her. For a few strides their
heads bobbed in time, then Bonny galloped
ahead as if winged and flew past the sagebrush.

I rubbed her neck, warm with sweat. "Good
girl! You know you're the fastest."

She galloped a second longer before settling into a jog. Elm mimicked her gait once he
caught up. I beamed proudly at Timere.

He laughed. "Alright—you won!"

"*Bonny* won," I corrected. "But Elm is
pretty fast, as well." I reached out to scratch
the gelding's mismatched forelock.

"He is," Timere agreed, knotting Grouch's
lead-rope to Elm's saddle horn again. "So,
where did you get 'Bonny' from?"

"I can't tell."

"I thought we agreed to trust each other."

"That doesn't mean we trust each other *completely*."

"I guess that will come with time?"

"Perhaps."

The horses walked leisurely now, nipping at one another's inside shoulders. I toyed with Bonny's mane, refusing to look Timere in the eye.

He didn't become angry, instead asking, "Shall we settle here for the night?"

I surveyed the wide, empty desert. "Yes. The sun will set—so it'll get cooler, and we can tie the horses to stakes."

We laid out our bedrolls and hitched the horses and mule to stakes in the ground. I untacked and rubbed Bonny down and let her roll. Then I checked her hooves and put her saddle on again. I noticed that Timere left Elm's saddle and bridle off.

"I'll put them on again in a little while," he explained. "Elm deserves a rest."

I smashed down the guilt that entered my

chest. Usually, I would leave Bonny's tack off, too—but I just couldn't risk it if Timere proved to be an enemy. He lit a campfire and offered me some bread, which I declined, wishing to finish off my own food first. When night fell, I lay awake.

What if Timere had wrong intentions for joining me on the way to Calico? What if he made a wrong move on me in the midst of the night? I shuddered and went to check on Bonny. She touched my cheek with her velvety muzzle. I buried my face in her mane. We were searching for a home—a place to stay and thrive in. What did Calico have to offer?

Taking a risk, I dragged my bedroll beneath Bonny so that her belly was over where my own stomach would be. She twisted her neck around to gaze inquisitively at this new setup, but stood square. I crawled into my bedroll, and she returned to swishing her tail at the summer gnats. Relieved, I drifted off to sleep.

Morning's light woke me at dawn. Timere had hunted quail for breakfast, and busied himself roasting them on a spit over the fire.

"Bonny stood still for you all night."

I grinned sheepishly and fastened my bedroll to the back of my saddle. "She's a good girl."

"I wouldn't hurt you, you know," Timere commented, his gaze intense.

How was it that he'd only known me for less than a day, and he could already read me so well? I drew up Bonny's cinch and fed her a handful of grain. She stamped her hoof impatiently and nose-knocked me. Timere offered me some quail, which I accepted gratefully.

When he continued to give me the cold shoulder, I apologized, "I'm sorry I'm so wary of you, Timere. I don't know whom to trust, and I hardly know you."

"It's alright," he dismissed me. "So, where did you come up with a name like 'Elizabeth Badger', anyway? Would you like me to keep using it when we're in public?"

"Please do," I grinned. "A relative of mine has the last name Badger. And Elizabeth is a common name in this day and age. I supposed no one would suspect it. Is 'Timere Westcott' *your* real name?"

Timere grinned in return. "Yes. My mother named me 'Timere.' 'Timere' means 'fearless' in the Latin language. My mother loved to read, and found my name in a book that she owned. The children at school used to call me 'Tim's Ear' because they thought my name extraordinary."

"It *is* extraordinary," I mused. "But in a good way."

He smiled and rose to feed Elm. I combed Bonny's mane with my fingers before swinging into the saddle.

"Can we go far today?" I hoped. "We're so close to Calico..."

"Why do you want to go there?" Timere wondered.

"I want a place to call home."

CHAPTER FIVE

We trekked a full twenty miles. I noticed Bonny was growing thinner, and I worried for her as I stripped her saddle off that night. Rubbing her barrel, I could feel her ribs closer to her skin than before.

"I'll give you extra grain tomorrow morning," I promised. "And we won't do as much galloping. We should be far away from Aunt Gertrude by now."

She only sighed contentedly and rolled.

This time, I left my bedroll on the opposite side of the campfire Timere set up.

"So," I said. "Why do *you* want to go to Calico?"

"There's silver," Timere responded—as if that should have been obvious all along. "If I can collect a good amount of it, I'll be rich."

"But it's been there for more than 13 years now."

"So?"

"So don't you think most of it will be gone by the time we get there?"

"No, or else everyone would be leaving. And there's *lots* of silver, I'm sure of it."

"Do they allow girls to mine?" Perhaps if I got hold of some silver, I could buy a house for Bonny and me, and afford food.

"I highly doubt it," Timere said seriously. "And it's dangerous in the mines. I'll bring back some silver for you."

"You will?"

"Why wouldn't I?"

I fell silent for a spell. "You'll bring me back *real* silver?"

"As real as your silver necklace."

I clutched at my round pendant. "This was my mother's."

"I'm not going to take it from you," Timere

chuckled. He paused. "Look straight at the fire again."

I frowned and shot him an inquisitive look, but obeyed.

"Your eyes turn bright gold when you do that," Timere commented. "They look like they have fire *in* them."

I blushed and chuckled forcefully. "Maybe they do! My aunt always called me a hell-bent little spitfire."

"You have the same color eyes as a coyote."

"That's how I've always thought of them," I blurted, unsure of what to say.

My eyes were a strange gold-brown— almost amber. They resembled that of a coyote's—nearly.

The fire crackled and shimmered. I scooted away from its heat. I'd never trusted anyone except John in my life. I rather wanted to share my past with Timere—but I was running away from that past. Talking about it only made the facts that John was dead and Aunt Gertrude might be searching for me all the more real.

Light shone in my eyes. I realized I had slept in. I stretched and hopped to my feet. Timere was feeding Elm, Grouch, and Bonny.

"Good morning," he greeted.

"Sorry I slept so long."

"You needed it," he dismissed me. "We're headed deeper and deeper into the desert—it'll be very hot."

I groaned. "I suppose Calico will be very hot then, too?"

"Hotter than that."

"We should get going, then."

"Don't you want breakfast?"

"I'll eat on the way."

Bonny loped eagerly when I finished eating and gave her her head. She and Elm attempted to race, but Timere and I held them back.

"I swear," I muttered to Bonny. "You'd run yourself to the death if you could."

She gave a spirited buck in reply. Elm, usually calm, yanked his head down, champing his teeth.

43

"Why are they acting like this?" I asked in frustration.

Timere turned Elm in a tight circle. "I think they smell other horses."

"But we're out in the middle of nowhere."

"Yah, I know." He pointed to some trees. "Just to be on the safe side, let's go hide over there."

"Bonny's nearly bright white…" I fretted.

"We'll cover her in a bedroll if needed."

We dismounted and led the horses over to the trees, ducking among them. Four men soon appeared on horseback, guarding a load-ed-down pack mule between them. Their faces were hard and grouchy.

"Bandits," Timere whispered.

I unfolded my bedroll and draped it across Bonny. She snorted—already hot enough—and I gripped the noseband of her hackamore to silence her.

The supposed bandits halted their horses so sharply that one reared to keep his balance.

"You said that there were people coming this way!" Bandit #1 snapped to Bandit #2.

"Yesterday, I saw an Indian boy and a girl down the road!" #2 protested. "Their saddle-bags were bulging, and I'm sure they were headed for the next town."

"But you didn't bother to pay attention to which direction they were going in," #1 argued. "Or to tell us you saw them."

"Let's forget it already!" Bandit #3 suggested. "There'll be more people coming this way, and we can get food and water from them. I'm hot and thirsty."

"But if we come across that boy and girl, I'll make them pay for causing me to look stupid," #2 said bitterly.

I pressed against Bonny.

"Shut yer trap!" Bandit #4 commanded in a thick southern accent. "I wanna get movin'!"

They spurred on their horses and slapped the pack mule's rump. They came closer and closer to our hiding spot. Bonny snorted at this and jerked her noseband out of my hands. I hurriedly yanked her head down, but it was too late.

45

The bandits halted their horses a second time.

"Did you hear that, boys?" #3 inquired.

"I think I did," #2 snarled happily.

Timere grabbed my arm and snatched me backward.

Bandit #2 dismounted his horse and squinted in the direction opposite of us. "Where are they?"

"I think yer bein' ridiculous!" #4 commented disgustedly.

"I agree," Bandit #1 said. "We've already been misled by you once. If it happens again, you'll greatly regret it. I promise you." #3 held up a hand. "Now wait a minute here—I heard a horse snort, too."

"It was probably yer own horse, ye dafty!" #4 insulted.

"Oh yah?" #3 threatened.

"Shut up, all of you!" #1 thundered. "I've had enough of your incessant jabbering! Let's move!"

They spurred their poor animals out of sight. I kept my breathing to a minimum for a full minute, until Bonny stamped her hoof and walked out onto the road.

I seized her reins and breathed a sigh of glorious relief. "Praise the Lord! Bonny, you are a bad girl! What were you thinking?"

She peeled back her lips to test the air, her ears rotating, then swished her tail and blew noisily through her nostrils. I traced my finger along the bright white stripe going down her bridge before folding up my bedroll.

"That was too close," Timere commented. "We'll need to be more careful as we get to Calico. Lots of robbers are hoping to steal any traveler's silver or gold. It's risky."

I nodded. "I just want to be there *now*."

"Our troubles won't be over once we are," Timere warned.

I tied my hair back and mounted Bonny. "I know. But being there will relieve my mind. Let's hurry and get moving. We're fortunate those bandits went in the opposite direction."

Timere hauled himself onto Elm's back and clicked to the gelding. We cantered a ways, then trotted to save the horses' energy.

"I think we'll reach Calico by tomorrow," Timere announced, putting away his map.

A smile lit up my dust-stained face. "I can hardly wait!"

The day wore on—the weather sweltering. Perspiration poured down the back of my neck. I had knotted my shawl beneath my chin to hide my hair, and set the old man's hat on top of it all. My unruly curls scratched the back of my neck and annoyed me, but I forced myself to ignore it.

My mother's pendant bounced against my chest to the stride of Bonny's trot. The only trees in sight were the thick, spiky Joshua trees, and they didn't offer much shade. It was too hot and dry to start a fire. When we stopped for the night, I drank some water from my canteen, grateful that I could refill it from the Mojave river. I mopped my sweat with my shawl and watched an owl swoop down, talons extended to snatch up its prey.

Bonny and Elm stood head to tail, warding insects from one another's faces. Grouch stood lazily, twitching his ears at some gnats. I stretched out on my bedroll, my hair spread out behind my head.

"What will we do when we get to Calico?"

Timere looked at me. "What do you mean?"

"Will we go our separate ways?" I emphasized, sitting up.

"Is that what you want to happen?"

"Not really," I admitted. I'd rather grown to enjoy and appreciate his company. "I have no one to stay with there, and I don't know exactly what I'll do yet."

The corners of Timere's mouth moved softly upward. "Then I suppose we won't go our separate ways," He frowned suddenly. "But I don't want you in the mines with me."

"Why not?"

"It's dangerous, Etta."

"How much more dangerous for me is it than for you?"

"You'd be surrounded by men, and rocks could fall down..." he set his jaw. "*Anything* could happen."

"You're not in charge of me," I raised my chin defiantly. "The reason I left the place I did is to find a home. But I also had no freedom there, and I value my liberty. Out here, I belong to no one but God, myself, the land, and the sky. I'll not let you tell me what to do."

"I'm telling you what *not* to do!"

"That's the same thing!"

"Why don't you just *listen*?"

"Why don't *you*?"

He stormed away from me to check on Elm. I lay on my side and tried to sleep. Minutes passed. Timere's bedroll rustled, indicating that he was settling down to keep guard. He'd told me that we'd perform a routine that night: taking turns watching for robbers. I listened to the horses shifting and occasionally whuffling softly.

"Timere?"

"Yah."

"I'll stay out of the mines if you really think it's unsafe."

"I do."

"I promise to stay out."

CHAPTER SIX

I jumped off my bedroll at the crack of dawn, despite having kept guard every two hours that night. Timere was still fast asleep, the top of his bedroll rising and falling with his shoulders as he breathed. I tacked up Elm and Bonny, and tied Grouch to Elm's saddle horn.

"We're headed to Calico today, girl and boys. We'll actually get there *today*!"

They nickered and thrust their muzzles into my palms. I laughed and prepared their grain. They each only received a little less than a handful—gulping it down and licking my palms clean—stamping when I offered no more. My own breakfast was a bit of hard bread. Timere and I really needed to stock up on supplies.

Elm disconnected from his stake in the midst of snuffling for weeds to crunch. He spooked at a lizard that skittered by and backed into Bonny by mistake. She rewarded the poor gelding with a bite on the buttocks. I lunged to grab his reins, but he was already trotting out yonder. Grouch managed to yank his lead rope free from the saddle horn, and returned to stand beside Bonny. I rushed after Elm.

"Easy, boy! Slow down!"

He flicked an ear in my direction, but never ceased trotting.

"Elm! Come back here!"

He swung round to face me, nostrils distended, ears pricked. At the worst possible time, a jackrabbit darted past. The gelding danced sideways, snorting. I managed to grab one of his trailing reins.

"Steady, boy. Hold still."

Elm bobbed his head and whinnied. Bonny answered him.

"Look at me, Elm."

As if he were able to understand, he looked at me. I stroked his bushy brown forelock.

"Steady."

He whuffled softly and lowered his head. I gathered both his reins and led him back to Bonny and Grouch.

Timere was awake. "You're good with horses."

"So I've been told," I replied. "But I think people just need to be gentle with them."

"I agree," Timere said. "Thank you for catching Elm." He patted the gelding's strong neck.

"You're welcome," I smiled. "Are you ready to go to Calico?"

The farther we rode, the more excited I became. I almost began singing to Bonny— when for the second time I remembered we weren't alone. Even the heat barely fazed me. Miles later, we pulled up the horses.

Timere pointed to some buildings in the far distance. "There's Calico."

My heart thumped so hard I thought it might pop out of my chest. Every step was one step closer to the place John had wanted me to chase my dreams to—one step closer to a possible home.

"I'm ready," I whispered. "Let's go."

CHAPTER SEVEN

I listened to the rhythmic sound of Bonny's and Elm's hooves hitting the rocky road. Voices clamored as we neared Calico. Suddenly, we were in the midst of the bustling mining town. It wasn't eye-catching or amazing, but it certainly was filled with dreamers. Men who hoped to become rich, and a few women and children here and there. Plenty of bearded men in all shapes and sizes. Calico seemed big with many buildings, but it was dry—so dry and sweltering.

Timere slid off of Elm, and I copied with Bonny. We walked side by side.

"What do you think?" Timere wanted to

know. "Is this the kind of place you'd want to call home?"

"I'm not sure," I confessed. "It's very big and crowded. But my friend John always said never to judge a book by its cover—nor a horse by its color."

"Especially if that color is *calico*?" Timere teased.

I elbowed him in the ribs. "Where are we headed?"

"Lane's General Store is a popular place here—run by a woman," Timere explained. "We'll get supplies there, or at the trading post."

"How do you know so much about this place?"

"I used to have a friend who'd been here before. He returned and told me about it—even drew me a map. A rough sketch, though."

We dodged people, horses, mules with carts, and even a yapping dog—finally reaching the general store. We hitched the horses to a post and stepped inside. It smelled sweet, foul, musty, and wonderful all in one. I followed Timere closely, unsure of how to act. I hadn't been in public since the town where "Jimmy" stole my money. I'd hardly spoken to anyone— save the old man and Albert Redfield. Before *that* I'd not been in public since I was ten years old. Being around people still troubled me.

I paused to gaze admiringly at a painting of a green field with the mountains in the distance, and a stream running through it all. When I looked up, Timere was gone. It troubled me more than I expected.

"Why lookin' so downcast, lass?" a tall man with missing teeth asked. The teeth that he did have were brown and seemed ready to fall out. His beard was tangled and gritty. "Do ye need company?"

"I—no." I was caught off guard. "Thank you for your offer, though."

He neared me slowly. "Ye look like ye could use company, pretty lass."

I jumped when a hand gripped my elbow. "She *has* company," Timere's voice said coldly.

The tall man backed away and shrugged. "Just tryin' to help," he tipped his hat and walked away.

Timere's eyes were hard as he stared after him.

"Sorry...." I began.

"I told you we'll have to be careful here. Come on," he barely looked at me, and I felt guilty for some reason.

Timere purchased food for us, along with a sack of grain for the horses. I used some of my savings to buy a sack of grain, as well. Elm, Grouch, and Bonny were going to be starving—the desert offered little forage except weeds and sage.

"What now?" I wondered as we loaded the horses.

"What were you planning on doing when you got here?" Timere asked.

"I was planning on finding work. My friend John suggested I help folks with obstinate equines. I'm not sure I'm needed for that, though. Perhaps I'll file hooves instead, for a low price. Speaking of which, Bonny will be needing her hooves done. How about Elm?"

"Well, he had shoes, but they wore off. His

hooves could use a filing. Do you think they'll be alright?"

"Sure. Bonny's never worn shoes in her life, and her feet are tough as iron."

Timere chuckled. "I want to work at Maggie Mine—where my friend did. I was thinking I could build us a shack near there. If I find work, of course."

"I like that idea. Let's find a place where you would build the shack."

Timere studied a piece of paper. "Maggie Mine is farther out. Let's ride the horses there, first."

We mounted Bonny and Elm. People stared curiously at me as we passed, and I blushed. Who could blame them? With my tattered dress, worn head-shawl, weather-beaten hat, and dirty-but-stunning mare, I was badly out of place.

Timere and I soon passed a saloon. Lively chortling emerged from its swinging double-doors.

"I hate how men go there with no intentions

other than to escape their own minds!" I said in disgust.

"I agree with you," Timere answered. "We'll both be sure to stay away from there."

I heeled Bonny into a jog. "Definitely."

Calico rested on a sort of plateau, from my perspective. We rode past the saloon, and came across a rickety building.

"That's Maggie Mine," Timere declared, a hint of pride and excitement in his tone. "I'll show you where I'd build the shack, then I'd better see if I can get work here."

We jogged the horses far from the mine. Here, the land dipped down a little, and the people and buildings could only be seen distantly.

"I think this would be a nice spot," Timere announced. "What do you think?"

I fell silent for a few seconds while looking around. Suddenly I noticed a crumbling shanty and a well. "Timere, look!"

He noticed them as well, and his features brightened. "I suppose I won't have to build that shack after all!"

We hopped down from the horses. I pushed

open the wooden door of the stone shack. It wasn't at all fancy, but I found I liked it. It had a wooden roof, a cooking area, and a small living space.

"Someone must have abandoned it," I remarked.

"I'm going to fix it up a little," Timere decided thoughtfully. "I don't want you sleeping in it until I know it's structurally sound."

He unloaded his luggage from Grouch. "Will you please watch all this for me?"

Certainly," I consented. "When will you be back?"

"As soon as I can. Do you have your pistol?"

"Yes."

"Wish me luck, then."

"May God be with you."

He cantered off on Elm.

I unloaded Bonny and drove stakes into the hard ground to tie her and Grouch to. They'd already been watered at a public trough. Bonny now nipped at her saddle.

"Not yet, girl. Wait for Timere and Elm to get back."

I found John's letter in my saddlebag and unfolded it, rereading it twice.

It was found more than thirteen years ago, and people from far and wide are flocking to the new mining town— men and women with dreams in their heads…I believe you to be fearless, Etta…Fate loves the fearless.

I missed John.

I brushed away my miserable thoughts and filed Bonny's hooves. I used my knife to pick her hooves clean, and to trim her tail and mane.

"Too hot to have all this hair, huh girl?"

Her tail was so long that it brushed the dirt. I sawed at it until it only reached the spots above her hind fetlocks. I only cut her mane a tiny ways above her shoulder. It was too pretty to remove too much of it. I threw out the hair for the birds to fashion their nests, and wove Bonny's mane into a thick, untied braid.

"You're so pretty, Bonny."

She flipped her braid to the other side of her neck and nuzzled me. I hugged her. Hoofbeats sounded, and Timere arrived with Elm, who now carried mining tools at the back of his saddle.

"I get to work at Maggie Mine!" Timere yelled triumphantly. "I bought tools, so now we're low on money, but I'll soon fix that."

"That's incredible, Timere," I praised him. "When do you begin work?"

"Tomorrow. I'll work in the mine five days a week."

"Are you pleased?"

He drove a stake into the ground and tied Elm to it. "Very. So this means I can fix up that shack. I'll start on it as soon as I can. Meanwhile, I think we should plant a garden. It would be a good way to get food in order to save money."

I allowed realization to dawn on me. "The ground is so hard…"

"We'll manage it." He handed me a shovel. "Shall we start now?"

63

I grinned. "As soon as the horses are untacked."

"Digging" in the dry, cracked ground was more like "banging." Our pickaxe and shovel hit the dirt over and over, yet the dirt remained stubborn. Timere insisted, that for a garden, he wanted to till the dirt and add fertilizer before planting anything. I risked taking off my shawl and using it as a bandana. Timere had his sleeves rolled up and his brows furrowed.

"You were right about the ground being so hard," he admitted. "This will take a long time."

I leaned dizzily on my shovel. "It's getting dark. I'll work on this tomorrow while you're at the mine."

We spread out our bedrolls. I read my book until it grew too dark to see, and watched the stars come out. Elm knelt at Bonny's feet, his eyes closed. She nibbled a weed nonchalantly.

Timere was studying his map of Calico. He glanced at me. "Hey Etta, remember when you said you don't know whom to trust?"

"Yes…" I said carefully.

"Do you trust *me* now?"

"I really don't know, Timere."

"Etta, I'd never hurt you."

I pushed my fingers into my snarled hair. "I hate to put it this way, but how can I know that for sure? How can *you* know for sure that *I'm* to be trusted?"

"I can't."

"Then why do you trust me?"

"Because we can't go through life not trusting anyone unless we know for darn sure they can be trusted," he said matter-of-factly. "Even those closest to you—those you trust completely—can turn out to be traitors. I'd know that firsthand. But if you never trust anyone, you'll never know what trust feels like. Maybe you're not trustworthy, Etta Alby, but I'm choosing to trust you. Even if that's wrong, at least I'll know what trust feels like."

Tears streamed down my cheeks. "I *don't* know what trust feels like," I whispered.

I'd never even fully trusted John—always expecting him to turn on me at some point. I was always on guard—always expecting the worst.

"Do you trust Bonny?" Timere asked simply.

"Yes…"

"That's a start." He touched my arm. "Trust doesn't have to come quickly. I'm awful sorry if I'm acting impatient with you."

I wiped my eyes. "*I'm* sorry I'm so stubborn. Let's get some sleep. We both have lots of work to get done tomorrow—with me tilling soil for the garden, and you working at the mine."

I lay awake a while longer—dwelling on my companion's lecture. I wanted to know what trust felt like.

CHAPTER EIGHT

W hen I awoke the next morning, Timere, Grouch, and Elm were gone. I discovered Timere's map of Calico beneath my hand with a note scrawled across the back: *Gone to the mine. I'll be back as soon as I can.*

I ate a meager breakfast and used a rag soaked with water to rub down Bonny. Having worn no saddle all night, she seemed in a pleasant, yet energetic mood, nibbling my hair and nuzzling me. Her coat was so dirty—a dull grey now, and her mane cascaded down her neck, tangled in knots—despite my many efforts to comb it with my fingers. Why hadn't I thought to pack a brush? I slung my saddlebags across

Bonny's withers and rode her bareback to the public trough, just to get some of her energy out. There, I filled my canteen and she sipped water.

We returned to our camp so I could continue the garden. Bonny crunched weeds while I dug. I folded my shawl, wet it, and tied it around my head so that it cooled my forehead and the back of my neck. Since the sleeves of my dress were already tattered, I tore them completely off midway to my elbows on my upper arms. My pickaxe pounded the dirt in a rhythmic manner, and sweat poured down my face. For two hours I toiled, the sun practically boiling my skin.

Bonny head-butted me between the shoulder-blades. She was thirsty and weary of standing in the sun. We made a second trip to the public trough, and I draped my bedroll across her withers when we returned. It wouldn't cool her off, but it *would* prevent sunburn, and the flies from biting her back and neck.

"I'm sorry it's so hot, pretty girl," I murmured.

She pressed her forehead to my chest, and my heart burned with affection at her enduring forgiveness and loyalty. All throughout the day I struck the ground with my pickaxe and tilled dirt. Bonny and I made several trips to the public trough.

On one trip, a beautiful young woman offered me a hairbrush. I'd forgotten to hide my hair with my shawl, and it sprung around my cheeks. I used the hairbrush on my own hair, which got so poofy I had to wrangle it into a braid. I also brushed out Bonny's mane and tail until they gleamed. My arms were sore from all this, and I ate dinner sitting underneath Bonny before digging again.

The sky shone blue and hazy overhead. Lizards sunned themselves on rocks. A roadrunner strutted proudly with a gopher snake in its beak. I leaned lazily on my shovel, my eyes closing from exhaustion.

The next thing I knew, someone was shaking my shoulder. It was becoming dark.

"Etta, wake up."

I yawned and looked about myself. I was

slumped on the ground with the shovel propped beneath my arm.

"You fell asleep," Timere chuckled. His brows furrowed suddenly. "Etta, your arms are all red."

I hopped to my feet. "I'm fine. Did you receive good pay?"

"Hardly any. The boss gave me a bit of silver to cash. I traded Grouch for some extra provisions. You can buy any other necessary supplies tomorrow."

"I'll buy soap, a bucket for the well, and seeds for the garden. A kind woman gave me a hairbrush today. I know it isn't considered sanitary, but I used it on Bonny as well as myself. You and Elm are welcome to it."

Timere busied himself rubbing down Elm. "Thank you. The miners liked Elm. All they have are donkeys and mules. Most sold their horses. I suppose the sensible thing to do would have been to sell Elm and keep Grouch, but I just can't lose him. I raised him from a colt." He stroked the gelding's neck, and Elm nuzzled him. "I'm sorry I took so long to return," he added.

"I kept busy."

"You did well."

"I'll find work once the garden is finished."

"And *I'll* try to return earlier tomorrow so I can begin fixing the shack."

My toil the following day was painstaking, but finally the dirt was soft enough to plant seeds.

"Bonny! The dirt's ready for planting! Let's go buy seeds and a bucket for the well!"

I threw my arms around her neck in a hug and climbed onto her bare back using a boulder. I reached forward and removed her hacka-more—that's how elated I felt. We galloped to Lane's General Store, where I purchased seeds, soap, a tin wash tub for bathing, and a smaller bucket to draw water. Timere owned a rope to attach to the smaller bucket.

Many people cast odd glances at me as I placed the small bucket, seeds, and bar of soap in the tin wash tub, and set it in front of me on Bonny, but I paid them no mind. Bonny and I strolled back to camp.

Within the next week, Timere repaired the shack for us, and we finished planting the vegetable garden.

I found work sweeping the Sweet Shop, which wasn't far from our setup. I bathed every two or three days inside the shack—filling the wash tub with water from our well. The brush began to wear out fast—with four living creatures using it. I pulled thick masses of coppery, black, blond, white, and brown hair from it each day. It was Christmas for the birds!

Autumn arrived, and the days grew steadily cooler. A few people paid me to file their horses' hooves. One morning, with nothing better to do, I walked to the Boot Hill cemetery. There were *so* many graves—some without names.

I was wandering down the line of headstones when one particular name caught my eye. I fell to my knees beside the headstone and gasped.

John James Badger
1829-1894
Was shot and buried in this very spot.

I breathed in great gulps that shook my entire body.

My stepbrother John died yesterday. Aunt Gertrude had said. *I just received word of it. He grew very sick.*

Shot and buried in this very spot.

Aunt Gertrude had lied to me. If John had died of sickness and she had just received word of it the day after, he couldn't have been shot at Calico. It would have taken a week or so for word to reach Aunt Gertrude from Calico of John's death. That meant that she must have known he'd been shot, and thought up a lie to feed to me.

I shook my head in disbelief and stormed from the cemetery, nearly crashing into a middle-aged man with a clean-shaven face.

"Are you Etta Alby?" he inquired.

CHAPTER NINE

I touched my necklace, glad I'd remembered to wear my shawl. "I beg your pardon, sir?"

"Is your name *Etta Alby*?"

"Why no. I'm Elizabeth Badger. Just ask anyone in town."

"How coincidental," he mused. "The woman that sent me to search for Etta Alby is Miss *Gertrude* Badger. Perhaps the two of you are related somehow."

"Perhaps."

"My name is Francis Quimby. Nice meeting you, Miss Badger."

"Nice meeting you as well."

"I wish you well. Please let me know if you come across an Etta Alby."

"I will be sure to. Goodbye, Mr. Quimby."

"Goodby, Miss *Badger*."

He emphasized my alias last name just as Timere had, but I thought I detected a sneer in *his* tone. I hurried all the way back to camp. Aunt Gertrude was looking for me. And she knew I might be in Calico. I trudged toward the shack. Bonny was nowhere to be seen, but her stake was still in the ground.

"Bonny!" I called.

The words scarcely left my mouth when I caught sight of the shack. The door was ajar. I stepped inside. Timere's and my things were in disarray across the floor, strewn everywhere. I thanked the Lord nothing was missing, and that Timere and I always kept our money on us. Someone had stolen Bonny, and searched through the shack for more to take.

John had been shot.

Aunt Gertrude was hunting me down.

Bonny was gone.

One terrible event after another began to

75

overwhelm me. I hadn't come this far only to be defeated. Tears threatened to spill, and I picked up Timere's extra belt on the floor, buckling it around my waist and tucking my daddy's pistol into it. I needed to find Timere and tell him Bonny was gone. I hung my water canteen onto the belt, knotted my shawl securely under my chin, and set off to walk to Maggie Mine.

The sun beat on my back, but my heart felt as though it was carved of stone. I arrived at the mine with a cold expression hidden by my dust-stained cheeks. I approached a man with a sway-backed mule and rickety cart.

"Pardon me, sir," I said. "I'm looking for Timere Westcott."

The man tugged at his sun-bleached beard. "I heard of him, ma'am, but I don't know where he is."

"Will you please help me find him? I need to speak to him badly."

"I'll ask Andrews if he seen 'em." He stomped off with his obedient mule in tow.

I waited 5 minutes, then 15. Impatiently, I searched for an entrance to the mine. A ladder descended down, and I took the chance. Instantly, pounding hammers, clanging shovels, and scraping pickaxes echoed through the underground. I trailed after the noise.

Shirtless, sweating men with muscles bulging in their arms paused in their toil to stare at me. I avoided eye contact, straining to see Timere—or at least Elm. I walked carefully down the tunnel before asking a man with a pleasant countenance about my friend.

He nodded with a smile. "Yes, I know Timere. Are you sweet on him or somethin'? It's dangerous for a girl to come down into the mines."

I ignored the teasing question. "Please take me to him."

The man led me round a couple corners until I spotted Timere. He wore no shirt, revealing his lithe upper body, and sweat covered his forehead and chest. He raised his pickaxe to strike rock, when my companion shouted, "Westcott! This here girl's been begging me to take her to you. You got somethin' you wanna talk about?"

Timere's face hardened when he saw me, and he picked up his shirt to clean his sweat. He put the shirt on and stomped over to me. The man left us alone.

"Etta, I told you—"

"Someone stole Bonny," I interrupted. Against my wishes, tears slipped from the corners of my eyes. "And my aunt lied to me, and this man found out my real name…"

Timere's hands moved up and down my arms. "Slow down. Start from the beginning."

"Bonny's gone."

"Are you sure she didn't just run off?"

"Someone was digging through all of our things. They didn't steal anything except Bonny."

"What's this about someone lying to you and finding out your real name?"

"Timere, I'm from Rancho," I explained. "I'm an orphan and I've lived with my cruel great-aunt all my life. When my friend John died, she told me he'd been very sick, and she said she was going to sell Bonny. John left a letter saying I should travel to Calico, so I'm here now. But I visited the cemetery today, and I found John's grave marker. It said he was shot and buried in the same spot. This man asked me if my name was Etta Alby, and I told him no, and we went our separate ways. But he doesn't believe me, Timere. He's working for my aunt to find me. I don't want to go back to her…"

"Calm down," Timere murmured, his eyes soft. "I'm not going to let anyone hurt you or take you away. Come on, we'll find Bonny." He paused. "Stay here, I have to go get Elm. A boulder crashed down and he's being used to haul it out of the way. I'll be right back."

The fact that I'd just shared my background with someone sank in. I felt slightly exposed, but also as if a burden had been taken off my shoulders. I knew what trust felt like.

Timere returned with Elm saddled. We exited the mine and sat double on the gelding.

"You can hold my belt," Timere ordered. "Speaking of which," he mentioned as we loped along, his tone a bit mischievous. "Why are you wearing my spare?"

"I needed it," I answered dully.

"We'll find Bonny, Etta."

"I hope so. Thank you for stopping your work to help me."

"You're welcome."

We reached the shack. I held Elm's reins while Timere inspected everything.

"I'm going to kill whoever did this," he fumed, looking so serious that I stepped backward.

Timere fastened his gun to Elm's saddle, and we sat double again on the patient gelding.

"We're going to ask around about Bonny," Timere announced. "Someone is bound to have seen her."

We asked around town, but no one had sighted a great grey-white mare with a flowing mane. I worried silently. Bonny was my best friend. I couldn't bear to lose her.

"There's no possible way someone could have brought her through town without being noticed," Timere said as we discussed the situation.

"Then the thief must have taken the back

way—or just went down the side of the plateau," I concluded. "But how will we find that person?"

"We'll think of something. It's Sunday tomorrow. I don't have to work in the mine. We also have to worry about that man who confronted you about your name."

I pulled at my hair. "I know. If he comes across me again, he may take me to my aunt."

"I will *not* let that happen," Timere assured me fiercely.

We ate dinner and went to bed. I listened to the night noises and Timere's soft sighs, worrying for Bonny until I dozed off.

BAM!

I sat up, startled.

BAM!

Something slammed against the shack door.

Chapter Ten

Timere grabbed his gun. It was still night. He cautiously opened the shack door.

There stood Bonny in her hackamore, her coat stained and her mane wild. There were whip-welts across her flank, and she whinnied at me. I rushed forward to embrace her tightly.

"*Bonny*! Where in tarnation have you been? I've been so worried about you!"

Bonny struck the ground with her forehoof, grunting impatiently.

"I'll fetch her water," I told Timere.

He took Bonny's reins from me while I lit a match and drew water from the well. As soon as my horse had drank her fill, she and Elm exchanged breaths and brushed noses.

"I'll have to give her a bath tomorrow," I laughed, shaky with relief.

"You have one smart mare!" Timere complimented. "Whoever stole her sure had a difficult time controlling her. She must have escaped."

"I'm so glad she did." I kissed Bonny's cheek. She rested her chin on my shoulder. "That's one problem solved."

The following day, Timere and I bathed Bonny and Elm, and I filed their hooves. At that moment, a small coach drawn by two horses stopped in front of us. *Francis Quimby* stepped out of it, his gleaming white teeth revealed with his icy smile.

"I've come for Miss Etta Alby," he announced, gesturing to me.

Timere's expression was daunting. "No Etta Alby lives here. You're mistaken."

"But that's Etta Alby standing right beside you," Mr. Quimby scoffed. "Your aunt has missed you, Miss Alby. Come along."

I planted my heels firmly in the ground, panicking. How could I get out of this? "I already told you, Mr. Quimby, I don't know of any Etta Alby. We met yesterday—you and I—you know very well my name is Elizabeth Badger."

The man's expression was now irritated. "I hate to take such drastic measures—but since you are failing to cooperate, I'm afraid I must." He pointed his gun at Timere. "You, move out of the way."

Timere's own gun was up at the shack, but he still refused to move. "You have no right to barge in here and command her to go with you. The marshal can arrest you for kidnapping."

Before another word was uttered from any of us, there was a loud BANG! Elm squealed, and Bonny tossed her head. Timere was on the ground. I was about to rush over and make sure he was alive, when a solid object crashed against my skull, and the world went black.

My head felt clouded over. I shook it repeatedly and surveyed my surroundings. I was in a coach. Why? Was I dreaming? Then it all came flashing back. Francis Quimby. The gunshot. Timere on the ground. Despair surged through me. Was Timere dead? I was going to *murder* Francis Quimby.

I banged on the front wall of the coach. "Let me out! Now!"

He either failed to hear me, or deliberately ignored me. I banged a second time, then tried thumping with my heels. After a few minutes, the coach stopped. The door opened.

"You're spooking my horses," Mr. Quimby complained. "You'll be let out as soon as I get you to your aunt."

"I'm not going to my aunt."

"Yes, you *are*—I'm following her orders whether you like it or not."

"Because she's offered you a large sum of money?"

"Exactly."

"You are a fool."

The door slammed shut again.

I emitted a huffed breath and slumped against the velvet seat of the coach as it began moving again. I needed to get out of here—away from Mr. Quimby. But how? At once, I remembered the knife from John. I always carried it in my pocket. Sure enough, it was there. I would escape somehow—using this knife—but I wouldn't truly murder Mr. Quimby—as furious as the hate boiling in my chest for him was.

The hours dragged on. There were no windows in this coach, so I couldn't see what time of day it was or where we were. It was maddening. At last, we stopped, and Mr. Quimby opened the door.

He bound my wrists with rope. "Your aunt warned that you're a wild one. No use taking any chances. Come along."

We walked into a cluster of trees. After fastening a rope around my waist and knotting it to a tree, he tended to the horses and started a fire. I refused to eat the dinner he offered me.

"Why did you shoot my friend?" I accused him hatefully.

"Don't use that tone with me. I merely injured him."

"How do you know he's not dead?"

"I don't. But I'm sure he'll be fine. It's not like that will matter to you anymore—you won't ever see him again after I return you to your aunt."

"I told you," my nostrils were practically flaring as Bonny's did when she was angry. "I'm not *going* to my aunt."

Mr. Quimby sighed dramatically. "Enough of your jabbering. I'm trying to enjoy my meal, and I don't want it ruined simply because I'm arguing with you when there's nothing to be argued over."

I fell silent and walked as many circles around the tree as my rope would allow, and then back again. Once my captor fell asleep, I would cut my bonds and figure out how to get back to Calico. Come to think of it, I didn't even know where we were—but we couldn't be too far from the mining town.

Mr. Quimby spread out some blankets and

came over to me. "I will do everything necessary so that you will not escape."

With that, he hammered a stake into the
trunk of the tree—directly above my head
where I was standing. I glowered brutally at
him as he slung my bound wrists over the stake
and knotted them to it. How was I supposed to
cut myself loose now?

All night, I dozed for less than an hour at a
time before waking up again. My mind plotted
ways to escape, and my arms grew sore from
remaining in the same position for so long. I
worried for my friends at the shack, and fretted over the fact that I might actually be on my
way to Aunt Gertrude. My mind circled from
one thing to another.

By morning, my wrists were raw, my arms
and back aching, and my spirit wilder than
ever. I refused breakfast from Mr. Quimby,
despite my rumbling stomach.

"You have quite the spirit," he marveled,
as I was wishing I could burn a hole through
him with the contempt in my eyes. "I'm sure
your aunt will break it out of you."

"Trust me, she's spent all my fifteen years of life trying," I snarled.

"Interesting."

When I ignored him, he ceased speaking. He hitched the horses to the coach and loaded me in. I thumped on the door to find it locked. I'd have to escape when we were outside. I fingered my knife and kissed my mother's pendant for luck. The day dragged on.

In spite of the cool autumn weather outside, the inside of the coach was hot, and the velvet seats played no role in preventing that. Twice I banged on the front wall for Mr. Quimby to give me water.

That night, as he tied me to a tree, I complained in a high-pitched voice, "My arms were sore last night when you staked them up! I'm going to tell my aunt you failed to treat me as a lady!"

Mr. Quimby sighed. "Very well. I'll leave your hands down, but your wrists will be bound more tightly."

I flinched as he secured my wrist ropes in place. Blood trickled across my knuckles. It

seemed to take forever for my captor to pre-
pare his bed, eat a dinner I also accepted, and
tend to the horses. Finally, the low rumble of
his snores reached me. Now I would escape.

CHAPTER ELEVEN

I sawed at my ropes quietly but quickly, ever-alert to the danger of my captor awakening. He snored on, fortunately. My ropes were thick and tight—and my knife once nicked me painfully. At last, I managed to cut myself loose.

I shoved some of Mr. Quimby's food into my dress pockets, and stole one of his canteens of water, doing my best to move silently. My heart nearly burst forth from my chest when Mr. Quimby grunted and rolled over. Luckily, the snoring sounded up again. I sucked in a deep breath and considered taking one of the horses, but that was going too far.

I crept out into the night. Suddenly I

realized that this location seemed familiar in the light of the moon. I was near a town. I walked farther out. I immediately recognized the general store, outside of which I had met the acquaintance of Albert Redfield. I knew where I was! And I was sure I had enough money to hail a stagecoach that would take me on a two day's journey. That could get me near to Calico.

At first, I had trouble finding a stagecoach driver willing to escort me. My appearance disgusted men who were used to proper young ladies. I reached an area near Calico in the dead of night. After paying and thanking my driver, I trudged the long walk to Timere's and my shack.

The moonlight guided me. Calico was eerily beautiful at night, I realized. A dog lifted his head to gaze at me as I passed. Recognizing me, he licked his chops and rested his chin between his paws again. A donkey extended his neck toward me, and I massaged his big ears. The place seemed like a ghost town—except for the animals and few lit windows. The buildings loomed like ships on the misty sea.

At the shack, Bonny and Elm were dozing head-to-tail. They nickered shrilly at my arrival. I buried my face in Bonny's mane and breathed in her horsey scent, and kissed Elm's forehead before hurrying to the shack. My heart thumped faster than my feet flew. If Timere wasn't alive…

I pushed open the shack door. Because of the moonlight, I could see the two bedrolls spread across the floor. *Timere* slept peacefully on his own—*alive*. I released a breath I didn't know I'd been holding. Perhaps the bullet hadn't hit him at all—perhaps he'd just hit his head on Elm's hoof when the gelding had reared in fright, and the impact knocked him out cold.

If I recalled the date correctly, Timere had to work at the mine tomorrow. I decided not to wake him, and settled onto my own bedroll. I lay awake, thinking hard. Mr. Quimby would most likely be looking far and wide for me. He probably knew I'd return to Calico. That meant

I wasn't safe yet. I felt underneath the portion of my bedroll that supported my head, where I always hid my pistol at night. Sure enough, it lay there.

Timere shifted nearby me. He was awake. "Who's there?"

"Me," I answered sheepishly. "I wanted to let you sleep…"

It was too dark in the shack to see him, but I imagined his dark eyes widening.

"Etta, do you have any idea how darn worried I've been?" Timere's voice was stern, and it sounded as if he were searching for a match. Seconds later, he lit one. "You look pale."

"*You* look pale!" I scoffed.

"I'm sorry I didn't go after you. That man shot me in the leg, and the marshal wouldn't let me leave town. He sent one of his men after you."

Now I really *was* pale. "So the bullet *did* hit you. I was so worried—I saw you on the ground and thought you might be dead."

Timere's match burned out. "I suppose we're even now."

I couldn't help it—I hugged him. "I'm so sorry he did that to you."

"I'm fine," Timere chuckled. "We should both get some sleep. Is your pistol near you?"

I grasped the barrel of my pistol even though I knew it was there. "Yes."

"Good. We need to be prepared if something happens tomorrow."

Timere was going to have an awful scar on his leg—I assumed from its condition. We were grooming the horses. I was so glad to be with Bonny again—for I hadn't ever been separated from her for four whole days since the moment we met.

When a stagecoach drawn by two horses halted a little ways from our shack, Timere and I exchanged wary glances, and he grabbed his gun.

An older woman stepped out the stagecoach, her nose wrinkled in disgust. A middle-aged man emerged behind her.

Aunt Gertrude and Francis Quimby.

I felt trapped. "That's my aunt, Timere. And she's with the same man who kidnapped me—Francis Quimby."

"It will be alright," Timere said soothingly.

But I noticed how he cocked his gun.

Aunt Gertrude strutted toward us, her posture poised and purposeful. She leaned on her parasol when she and Mr. Quimby reached us.

I clutched my mother's necklace. *Oh, dear God, please don't let her take me away.*

"It really *has* been a long time since I last saw you, Etta," my aunt greeted me icily. "I hear you have quite skillfully evaded Mr. Quimby, here."

I glared her full in the eye. "How did you find me?"

"Oh, I knew you had to be here, for this is where John lived. I suspected you were making sure he was dead," she informed me.

"So you admit it, then."

"I admit *what*, dear?"

"Don't you *dare* call me 'dear'!" I shrieked, spooking Elm. "You lied to me! I saw John's gravestone. I *read* his description. He was shot. Do you care to explain that, or shall I ask Marshal Bismark? Perhaps *he'll* know."

Aunt Gertrude's cheeks flushed. "Hold your disrespectful tongue, girl! What on earth are you implying?"

"That you arranged John's death."

"That is *quite* an accusation."

"Tell. Me. The truth," I growled between clenched teeth. "I deserve to know."

"You deserve nothing."

"And you *do*?"

Aunt Gertrude drew to her full height. "I am taking you home with me and selling that horse. This time, I *will* turn you into a proper lady. You owe it to me—"

"When have I ever owed you *anything*?" I shouted. "You feel no love for me! John loved me, and I loved him. Out of your cruel, love-less heart, you extinguished that flame. You're taking away everything I truly care about. You care for no one but yourself."

"*You* are an uncivilized little *rat*," Aunt Gertrude hissed. "It is *you* who doesn't know love—just like your mother didn't. Yes,

Etta—I lied to you. I have been lying to you your entire life—all for *your* well-being! How do you repay me? With ungratefulness! Your grandparents cast your mother out as a child. She met your father, and he cared for her until they married. *Then* do you know what occurred? He left her when she was pregnant with you, and you were sent to your grandparents. They cast you out just as they did your mother. No one ever loved you. *I*, out of my supposed 'loveless' heart, adopted you. I fed you and *attempted* to raise you properly. You are a rebellious little *mustang*—a *stray*. No one loves you, and no one ever will. Yes, I hired someone to shoot John. He filled your head with wild fantasies that no one should hear. And now that he is gone, things will run smoothly—as they should."

Tears streamed down my face. "I will never go 'home' with you. No place which contains your presence is home. I detest you!"

"So you wish to stay *here*?" she questioned. "You wish to live like a dog in a stone shack—doomed a scavenger all your days—living with a savage?"

For the first time since the fight occurred, I became aware of Timere's presence—and that of Mr. Quimby's. They were both bewildered beyond speaking ability.

"Yes," I responded quietly. "I wish to stay here. I never want to see you again."

"And so you shan't." She motioned Mr. Quimby into the stagecoach, and paused. "You are a shame to God Himself," she spat.

Then Aunt Gertrude Badger climbed into the stagecoach. The poor, dumbfounded driver cleared his throat and tipped his hat at me before popping his whip. The stagecoach disappeared.

CHAPTER TWELVE

I broke down sobbing, and collapsed.

Timere knelt beside me and pulled me close. "Hey… Not one thing she said is true. *None* of it."

I shuddered. "She was telling the truth about my grandparents and mother and all—I'm sure of it."

"But the rest wasn't true, Etta. Shh…It wasn't true." He waited until my sobs died.

I emitted a shuddery sigh. "I can't believe she would *kill* John."

Timere's face twisted painfully. "John was your love?"

I gazed at him in surprise, breaking free of

his arms. "Timere, John was practically an old man! He was Aunt Gertrude's stepbrother. He gifted me Bonny and taught me to ride her and file hooves. We weren't in *love*!"

Timere scratched the back of his neck and stood. "I just heard you say…"

"Yes, I loved John, but not in *that* manner!" I tore off my shawl and changed the subject. "I guess I won't be needing this anymore. I can tell folks the truth now." I paused. "You know, Aunt Gertrude was right about one thing."

"What's that?"

"I *am* a mustang—a stray," I said. "You know those wild horses that run like the wind and have hearts like fire? The best ones refuse to be tamed—they just want to run unbridled all their days. I should like to be compared to them."

Timere smiled. "You are definitely a mustang. You are just as free-spirited and defiant as they."

I smiled back, then scowled. "I'm terribly sorry she called you a savage, Timere. You're *not*. That's an awful name."

My friend grinned mischievously. "Aren't savages people who are uncivilized and wild? I should like to be compared to them."

We laughed.

It was wonderful to be called Etta Alby again, and wonderful not to always wear my shawl. People began to call on me more regularly to tend to the hooves of their equines, a task they paid me for. I went back and forth from job to job as the citizens of Calico discovered my "talent" with horses. I broke a young colt to saddle, worked with a mare who refused to lift her feet for anyone, and calmed a miner's donkey that spooked at clanging metal. I enjoyed all of this immensely, but it sometimes clashed with my other duties.

Timere was free from the mine Wednesdays and Sundays. While he was away, I tended the garden, continued my tasks at the Sweet Shop, and bought necessary supplies for Timere and me. I also cleaned the shack and took Bonny for bareback gallops.

One miner built us an outhouse in exchange for me gentling his kicking mule. Timere also constructed a small corral for Bonny and Elm. These were our luxuries out in the desert.

I turned sixteen before autumn changed into winter, and the air grew as sharp as Bonny's nips. I was grooming Bonny one afternoon when the town Marshal rode up on his big buckskin gelding. I waved, confused as to why he would visit us.

Marshal Bismark Bob dismounted his gelding. "How are you, Etta?"

"Fine, marshal," I said cautiously. "What brings you here?"

He removed his hat. "Etta, I'm afraid there's been an accusation made against you."

"What kind of accusation?"

"William Donovan claims you stole his prize stallion."

"The palomino named Loot?"

"That's the one."

I shook my head in disbelief. "Marshal, do you see a stallion in that corral? You can even check the shack and the outhouse—you won't find one. The only horses we've got are Bonny and Elm. Why would William Donovan accuse me of theft?"

The marshal scratched the back of his neck. "I don't know, Etta, but he says you were the last one to work closely with that stallion. Besides himself, of course."

"Simply because he had a biting habit I was paid to rid him of!"

"Donovan has high status in this town. Folks are believin' him—especially since you turned out not to be who we all thought you were. I'm just here to warn you, and to tell Donovan I didn't find his stallion at your place."

"Please tell Mr. Donovan I would never steal Loot," I requested. "He can even have his money back if he wishes."

"I'll be sure to mention that," Marshal Bismark promised. "Have a good day, Etta."

"Same to you, marshal."

He and his buckskin left.

"Can you believe that, Bonny?" I rambled to her. "William Donovan thinks I stole Loot!"

Bonny shook her mane and scuffed the dirt.

"Me neither," I pretended she was agreeing with me.

Timere came back from Maggie Mine that evening—and he wasn't alone.

A blond girl with big blue eyes accepted his help down from Elm. My heart thudded in my chest when she smiled sweetly at my best friend.

THEN do you know what occurred? He left her…

"Hey, Etta!" Timere greeted me. "This is Mary Wickham. She can't find her father, who works in Maggie Mine. She needs a place to stay, so I told her she could stay with us until she found him."

CHAPTER THIRTEEN

I forced a smile. "Hello, Mary. Are you hungry?"

"I would love something to eat, thank you." Mary's smile was white and sparkling. "It's nice to meet you, Etta. Timere has told me much about you."

"It's nice to meet you, as well," I agreed. "Here, Timere—I'll tend to Elm while you fetch Mary something to eat."

I practically snatched Elm's reins from a surprised Timere and led him to the corral. Bonny whinnied happily when she spotted the gelding, and they bumped foreheads.

"Elm didn't bring home a strange mare

to you, did he?" I grumbled sarcastically as I stripped the gelding of his tack.

He breathed across my cheek before bucking jubilantly and inviting Bonny to play. I watched them race the length of the corral and nip at one another.

When I entered the shack, Mary and Timere were leaning against the wall eating bread and beans. I joined them silently.

Timere broke the silence. "I'm going to sleep out with the horses. I have an old blanket, and Mary can use my bedroll."

I nodded.

Mary looked to the both of us. "Thank you for being so welcoming. I greatly appreciate it."

I smiled. "We're glad to have you."

I tried to feel glad. Mary was a sweet girl— so polite and ladylike. I had no right to bear hard feelings against her—or Timere. He'd done the right thing bringing her here.

I finished my meal. "I'm going to check on Bonny one last time before bed. I'll be right back."

"I'll go with you," Timere declared. "Will you be fine, Mary?"

She blinked her long lashes. "Of course. Go tend to your horses."

The minute we got outside, Timere scowled at me. "You don't seem very happy."

"What do you mean?"

"Don't play pretend with me, Etta. You won't look me straight in the eye, and you practically glared at Mary when I introduced the two of you."

"I'm terribly sorry I behaved that way. I'm suspicious of strangers."

"I don't think that's it."

"I'll treat her nicely, Timere."

"That's not what I mean." He stopped and faced me. "Hold out your hand."

I obeyed. He dropped a stone into my palm.

"I'll tend to Bonny and Elm. Go back to the shack," he said before storming off.

I examined the stone, only to become aware that it wasn't a stone at all. It was a small piece of silver hammered into a diamond shape. I stared at it a long moment.

I'll bring back some silver for you.

Timere had kept his promise.

I dropped the silver diamond into my pocket and entered the shack. Mary was unpinning her hair.

"Are the horses alright?" she wondered.

I nodded. "Last I saw, they were frolicking in their corral. I think Timere has decided to go straight to sleep out there."

"Does he love horses?"

"Yes, he does. He loves Elm."

"I can tell," Mary beamed. "When he was saddling Elm, he was so gentle with him! And he talks regularly to him."

I half-smiled. "Horses like to be talked to," I hesitated. "Mary?"

"Yes?"

"I apologize if I seemed unfriendly at your arrival. I'm suspicious of newcomers, and we've never had anyone stay with us before."

"I forgive you, Etta. It must seem as if I'm imposing upon your privacy. You have a right to be suspicious. I only wish I could find my father."

"But you're *not* imposing upon our privacy!" I protested. "There's nothing to be kept private. You're a nice girl, and we'll help you find your father."

I swear—she never ceased smiling. "Thank you, Etta. Now, let's be off to sleep before my eyes turn red instead of blue!"

The next day was Wednesday. Timere and Mary searched for Mary's father while I went to try and clear up the accusation against me. Timere and I hardly spoke to each other, and neither of us mentioned the silver diamond.

I was letting Bonny drink from the public trough before I reached William Donovan's house, when a young woman tapped my shoulder.

"I'm Victoria Wordsworth," she introduced herself in a clipped English accent. "You're Etta Alby, correct?"

"Yes," I replied. "Good day, Miss Wordsworth."

"*Mrs.*" she corrected me politely. "Please

listen: I'm only temporarily visiting my brother here in Calico with my husband, and we're leaving quite soon to return to England—but I heard about how William Donovan accused you of stealing his prized horse."

"What about it?" I asked guardedly.

Mrs. Wordsworth patted the pins in her wavy, multicolored blond hair. "Don't be so high-strung—I want to help you. I think I have a solution to your problem. I don't believe you would steal from anyone."

"I wouldn't," I agreed. "What is your solution?"

"I could ask Mr. Donovan how much he would have sold that horse for. He names the price, and I pay it. It's simple."

I shook my head so hard that some of my hair came loose from its barrette. "No—I couldn't ask you to do that. That stallion is of fine breeding and excellent stamina. He would cost hundreds—maybe even thousands!"

"I'm not giving you much of a choice," Mrs. Wordsworth declared bluntly. "I'm rich, for heaven's sakes! I may as well put my money to good cause."

I sighed. "First, please just wait awhile. The stallion may show sooner or later."

"Or never. But, I'll do as you wish. Good day." She bobbed a curtsy and hurried off.

Bonny and I rode to William Donovan's house, where I rapped on the door. He answered it himself, his ruddy face immediately hardening.

"*You*!"

"Yes, it's me," I greeted him. "Nice to see you too, Mr. Donovan."

"Where's my horse?"

"That's what I've come to speak to you about. I didn't steal Loot, Mr. Donovan. The marshal even inspected my property."

"You could have sold him!" the angry man accused, sticking a finger in my face. "Or hidden him!"

"If I had sold him, Timere and I wouldn't be so poor. If I had hidden him, I'd have to go out and feed him every day."

"I don't want to see you. I want my horse."

"Please, Mr. Donovan—"

The door slammed in my face. I glared at it and whirled around, only to see Victoria Wordsworth. Again.

Chapter Fourteen

"You didn't have much luck," she mentioned, blunt as usual.

"I'm glad you noticed," I said sarcastically.

"Don't be rude to me. I told you my way is best."

"You never said that. You said you weren't giving me much of a choice."

"That's exactly right. Consider my proposal as the townspeople continue to cast sour looks upon you."

"I've already considered your proposal ma'am, and I'm declining."

Victoria Wordsworth tilted her head and smiled regally. "I'm afraid I don't allow anyone to decline my proposals. I'll see you tomorrow, Mrs. Alby."

"*Miss*," I corrected.

Mary was crying when I returned home with Bonny. Timere's arm was around her shoulders.

"What's happened?" I wanted to know.

"We recently found Mary's father dead—by the saloon," Timere spoke low. "She wrote a letter to her grandmother to come for her."

I touched Mary's shoulder as she trembled with sobs. "I'm awful sorry, Mary. You can stay with us until your grandmother comes."

She nodded and dabbed at her eyes with a handkerchief, crying more earnestly.

I tended to Bonny and prepared dinner. Timere ate outside without thanking me. I gave Mary the privacy of the shack to bathe and change her clothes. Mary spent Thursday at the shack alone while I worked at the Sweet Shop until midday.

Victoria Wordsworth met me at the door when I started to leave for home.

"William Donovan has accepted my proposal," she told me proudly.

I glared at her. "We made a deal!"

"*You* suggested a deal, and I declined it. Surely you're aware that there are human beings more stubborn than yourself, *Miss* Alby?"

"You broke your word!" I fumed.

"Please—you should be thanking me. Mr. Donovan has agreed to take back his accusation and forget the whole ordeal. I told you—a little money goes a long way."

"A *little* money?"

"A little for me."

I sighed. "Fine. Thank you very much, Mrs. Wordsworth."

"Call me Victoria."

"Thank you, Victoria."

"You're welcome, Etta. Good day!" she practically skipped down the road.

I shook my head and almost crashed into William Donovan. He grinned widely at me. "Howdy, Etta!"

I raised my eyebrows. "Hello, Mr. Donovan."

He removed his hat. "I wanted to say I'm awful sorry for accusing you of stealing Loot. I know you wouldn't do such a thing."

"That's real kind of you, Mr. Donovan."

"I hope you harbor no hard feelings."

"Certainly not."

"Thank you kindly, Etta!" Whistling, he left me.

I wasn't sure whether to laugh or get out of there as soon as possible before he changed his mind. I swung onto Bonny.

"Bonny—folks are just plain crazy around here!"

Mary was quiet as I swept the shack floor.

"How are you feeling?" I asked gently.

"I miss my father, but that's not what I'm thinking about."

"Might I ask what you *are* thinking about?"

She looked me full in the eyes. "Etta, you and Timere haven't been speaking, and you've been avoiding one another. Is it because of me?"

"No, Mary—or course not!" I told her. "Timere and I have our ups and downs. Please don't fret over it."

A week later, Mary received word that her grandmother was on the way to fetch her—but it would take a while. Mary and Timere embraced over the news, and I felt a stab of jealousy against my will. I visited Bonny and Elm to soothe myself. They stood patiently as I hugged their necks and rubbed their muzzles.

"I came here looking for a home," I chattered to them. "Is that what I found?"

Elm lipped at my dress pocket for grain. I gently pushed his nose away.

"I'm confused, girl and boy."

Bonny shoved her forehead at my chest. I buried my face in her long mane and hummed. She and Elm both stepped back and swiveled their ears to catch the sound. I softly sang a poem I had made up out of boredom at Aunt Gertrude's place.

I love you like the moon, shining ever bright
I love you like a star, lighting up the night

I love you like a doe, swiveling her ears
I love you like God's hand, drying away the tears

I love you like a cat, cleaning off her hide
I love you like my soul, ever filled with pride

I love you like a horse, rearing to the sky
I love you like our Lord, warning us not to cry

I love you like the flame, burning in my heart
This is how I love you, and it's only just the start

Bonny tugged at some strands of my hair with her teeth. I kissed her pink snip and headed to the shack for dinner.

Little problems occurred that everyone noticed but no one discussed. Spring was coming. I'd started a garden that I hoped would produce well. The little problems lingered consistently. Elm limped slightly, so Timere walked to the mine. I considered lending him

Bonny, but she wouldn't tolerate all the clanging—much less being handled by strangers. Timere also wasn't bringing back as much money, either. Mary's grandmother seemed to be taking forever to fetch her granddaughter, and this worried Mary. Timere and I still barely spoke to one another.

One cool, Wednesday afternoon, Mary and I were eating pickles while Timere repaired the corral fencing. Carriage wheels rattled in the distance. It was a stagecoach, and an old lady with a sweet face like Mary's emerged from it.

"Grandmother," Mary breathed, and rushed toward her.

Timere and I walked over to watch. Mary embraced the old woman, and they both cried tears of joy.

"Thank you ever so much for watching over her," Mary's grandmother said, dabbing her eyes with a lace handkerchief. "I don't know what I would have done if she had been out here all alone—in the middle of nowhere."

Timere smiled. "We were glad to do it, ma'am."

Mary retrieved her carpet bag from the shack and loaded it into the stagecoach. Then she faced me. "I'm going to miss you, Etta."

"I'm going to miss you too, Mary," I murmured, and I meant it. Her lovely laugh, sweet smile, and our talks before bed—I'd miss it all. We hugged each other tightly. "Stay safe," I whispered.

"You do the same."

"Oh, and Mary?"

"Yes?"

"A friend of mine told me in a letter, 'Fate loves the fearless'. I thought you might want to remember that one. I have, and it's helped me."

She smiled. "I'll remember it."

She and Timere also embraced. She whispered something to him and he nodded. Just when Mary started to climb into the stagecoach, she whipped round and kissed Timere smack on the lips. Then she hurried to join her grandmother. The stagecoach rattled down the dusty trail, and that was the last I ever saw of sweet Mary Wickham.

Chapter Fifteen

Timere gazed after that stagecoach with a wistful look in his eyes. I went to check Elm's lame leg.

"You look better, boy," I commented as the piebald trotted toward me, nickering.

Timere and I had been soaking his ankle in cool water every day, and the fetlock area never swelled. I touched Elm's leg and felt no heat.

"I think you can go back to work at the mine tomorrow," I said, laughing when he bobbed his head as if to agree.

I leaned against Bonny and withdrew the silver diamond from my dress pocket, fingering it. Why did I care so much about whether

Timere was sweet on Mary or not? She was elegant and lovely—he had every right to like her.

"You know why I made that into a diamond shape?" Timere's voice startled me out of my reverie. This was the first time that he had looked me in the eye since the night Mary joined us.

"No—I don't," I stammered. Sometimes I felt as if he could hear my thoughts. He knew me too well.

"When a horse has a diamond marking we call it a 'star'," Timere explained. "You're always looking at the stars before bed."

"It's beautiful," I said finally. "Thank you for keeping your promise."

"Etta, I'm sorry I've been avoiding you."

"I'm guilty of the same thing."

"What happened?"

"Nothing, I'm just tired."

He searched my face. "What *happened*? With our friendship. Are we going to be honest with one another?"

I stared at my worn and tattered boots. "I hope so."

"Do you want me to begin?"

I nodded.

Timere sucked in a breath. "The way you acted when I brought Mary home made me angry—as if you suspected me of casting you away."

"For a moment, I did," I admitted.

All at once, his hands were moving up and down my arms as they had when I'd alerted him of my troubles at Maggie Mine. "I would never cast you out, Etta."

"I know."

He released my arms. "Now you can tell me your side of the story."

I faced my back to Timere. "I felt excluded when you brought Mary home. I felt cast aside, even though you didn't intend it. And Mary is so sweet and friendly…I wish I could have done more for her. I don't know why I acted the way I did."

"Same with me—about *my* actions."

"Timere…Are you sweet on Mary? She kissed you…"

"*She* kissed me, Etta—not the other way around," Timere protested.

"That doesn't mean—"

"Mary *is* pretty and ladylike, but she and I both know we could never be together."

"And if you *could* be together?" I turned to face him again.

"I *do* like Mary, Etta. A person can't change their feelings. But—"

"I should water my plants," I interrupted, staring past him. "And you've got the fence to mend." Without another word, I went to my garden.

"I'm terribly sorry," I apologized to Lucy Lane at Lane's General Store. "I'll pay you back for that grain as soon as I'm able."

It was spring, and Timere and I were in debt to Mrs. Lane for grain and soap.

I ran my hand along Bonny's barrel outside of the general store. "You're becoming thin, girl. I'm sorry I haven't been feeding you a proper amount."

On the trip to Calico, Bonny and Elm had received a handful of grain each morning, since they could graze all the grass they wanted at our rest stops. Here *in* Calico, the packed ground offered little but weeds. The horses relied on the edible plants they could find, and the large amounts of grain from Timere and me. We originally fed them twice a day, but now that was reduced to once a day because of lack of grain.

"We're in terrible debt to Lucy Lane," I told Timere that evening. "We owe her sixty dollars!"

He nodded, his face grim. "We'll pay her back. I'll find extra work for money."

We were avoiding an awful fact: Timere had developed a bad cough over winter, and it was worse now. He'd been taking a couple of herbs, but they barely helped. And I suspected the dank air of Maggie Mine wasn't improving his health, either. When I'd mentioned this, he'd gotten defensive.

We were both homely sights, as well. Timere's hair was even more scraggly and

126

longer now, so he began tying it back with a strip of leather. Not to mention that he appeared leaner from eating nothing all day from breakfast until dinnertime.

My own hair had grown terribly snarled and even longer—down to my rear end. It was so matted and hard to handle that Timere had trimmed it shorter. My clothes were wearing out fast, so a kind old woman gifted me a new dress.

She'd laughed and patted my cheek. "I figured I could spare you a bit of clothing, my dear—your clothes have been looking so ragged lately. I couldn't bear to see you that way!"

I spent the next week performing odd-jobs for anyone willing to hire me. I did laundry and took care of children.

Timere counted the money I earned that week one evening. "Added to what I've earned, we can pay back twenty dollars of the debt."

"We've only earned twenty dollars altogether?!" I was aghast.

"No—we can only afford to *spend* twenty

dollars—if we want to feed ourselves and the horses."

"Are we going to be alright?"

Timere eyed me sideways. "Why wouldn't we be?"

"You're sick—whether you'll confess it or not. We're hardly making any money. Bonny and Elm are skinny," I hesitated. "So are you, Timere. You've only been eating twice a day."

"I'm fine. We're going to be fine. Stop worrying. We'll pay off the debt, and your garden will produce vegetables."

Each morning while I fed the horses, I prayed for a miracle. *I've gotten this far, God. I can't stop now. I can't fail now.*

Early one spring morning, my prayers were answered.

PITTER-PATTER-PITTER-PATTER

Hundreds of tiny "objects" tapped on the shack roof. I yawned and sat up, pushing the door open a smidgen. At that moment, freezing air and water hit my face.

Rain.

CHAPTER SIXTEEN

"Timere, it's raining!" I shouted, throwing the door wide open and skipping outside.

Timere awoke as the rain spattered his face, too. Bonny and Elm paced the length of the corral, whinnying. I unlatched the gate, releasing them. They romped and reared in the mud, rejoicing in the glorious rain.

Timere exited the shack, hair pasted to his cheeks. "I can't believe it's raining!"

I spun in a circle, feeling as wild and alive as the horses. "Me neither! I haven't seen rain in so long!" I tilted my head back and let the rain wash down my face.

Bonny nickered and approached me. I gazed at her. She bobbed her chin and flung her fore-hooves out, splattering me with mud. I squealed a little with laughter, and grabbed a handful of mud, tossing it at her withers. She flung more at me. I seized a second handful and hit Timere square on the shoulder. He glared in mock fury and tickled me. I shrieked with laughter, toppling over sideways.

"*Timere!*" I launched more mud at him.

We were all going to need baths after this. Elm rolled, and Bonny shoved Timere off his feet. We frolicked in the rain and mud for a long while.

While Timere bathed in the shack, I scrubbed Bonny and Elm in the corral. They were in high spirits—pawing the ground and tossing their forelocks often. By the time they were clean, my arms ached.

Timere laughed when he exited the shack, prepared to ride Elm to the mine. "You're dirtier than you were the last time I saw you!"

I jabbed him with my elbow. "Your horse rolled in the mud when it was raining! It's never taken me so long to wash a horse before."

I was weeding my garden when Timere and Elm galloped home.

"I found silver, Etta!" Timere hollered loudly enough to scare all the birds clear out of Calico. "I've got lots of silver! I'm allowed to keep it!" He jumped from Elm's back while the gelding was still in midstride, and grasped my hand, dropping several objects into it. I stared at my palm.

"How much is this worth, Timere?"

"Enough to pay off our debt," he said excitedly. "I'll get it cashed."

I fingered the silver. It wasn't beautiful or sparkling—but it was an answer to my prayers. "This is incredible."

"I'll be back as soon as I can with it cashed," Timere said. "Then I'll go straight to Lane's General Store."

My garden produced a reasonable amount

of vegetables that year—but many of them shriveled and died in the heat of summer. I was really beginning to think of Calico as home. 1895 was a good year. I turned 17, and more people than ever hired me to file hooves and gentle the flaws of their equines.

In 1896, Calico began to change. The value of silver went down to $0.57 per troy ounce—much to Timere's fury. The population declined in number.

"It feels like everything is changing," I said to Timere one day as I picked Bonny's feet clean.

"Change is part of life," he replied matter-of-factly, scrubbing at Elm's saddle.

"I know—but that doesn't make it any simpler."

"Etta—the world isn't changing around you—you're changing *with* the world."

"I know."

Timere gently pried my knife from my fingers. "I want to show you something."

I followed him to the shack. He rummaged through his saddlebags, and faced me when he found something. "This was my mother's—like your necklace was *your* mother's."

As if to emphasize his point, my hand clutched at the charm of my mother's silver pendant.

Timere revealed an ornately jeweled hair clasp. "My mother hated change, as well. She was one of my closest friends."

"What happened to her, Timere?" I dared to inquire.

I'd never seen his expression so depressed. "My father poisoned her. I'll never know why. He just left after he did it. I wanted to *kill* him." The new fury that filled my friend's voice was passionate.

I touched his arm. "I'm so sorry."

"It's in the past. I promised myself I'd never dwell on the past anymore."

"I suppose you and I have something in common with our pasts: both our fathers betrayed our mothers."

"I suppose you're right. Do you want to keep the hair clasp?"

My eyes widened. "No—it was your *mother's*!"

"I want you to keep it."

"Timere…"

He moved behind me and fastened the clasp into my hair. "Please keep it. You look beautiful."

"It's lovely. I'll treasure it."

Suddenly, Bonny's scream pierced the air, followed by loud crackling.

I scrambled to my feet and ran as fast as able down to the corral. *The fence was on fire.*

Chapter Seventeen

"Bonny!" I screamed. She and Elm were pacing and trumpeting frantically.

I rushed forth, panicking. The gate was on fire…I needed to get it opened. Timere busied himself drawing water from the well. I grabbed the tin wash tub to assist him. The fire quickly spread to the outhouse. Smoke choked my lungs, but I made trip after trip to the well.

After we doused the gate with water, Timere opened it. Elm came racing out, his eyes rolling into his head. Timere threw his hands into the air and crooned to the fearful gelding.

"Bonny's still in there!" I cried. "I'll get her."

Timere reached for me. "Etta, don't you dare! The fire is spreading back over the gate!"

I swerved around him. "I need to get Bonny! I hear her screaming!"

"Etta—"

I darted through the gate. It slammed shut behind me. Smoke choked my lungs and burned my eyes, and I coughed violently, my vision blurring. Bonny was pacing frantically, calling for Elm. It was the first time in my life I'd seen her act insensibly.

"Bonny! We have to get out of here!"

She ignored me.

I lunged forth and hauled myself onto her back, heeling her hard. "Take us out of here, Bonny."

She raised her head high, ears pricked, nostrils distended. She whickered loudly.

"Bonny—we'll both die if we don't get out of here."

I dug my heels into her sides. She twisted her neck around to look at me, the intelligence and wisdom returning to her dark eyes. She half-reared and galloped straight for the gate. My heart thudded in my chest. Flames slowly flickered across it.

Bonny's stride steadied but never faltered. I clung to her mane. She gathered her haunches underneath her and pushed off with her hocks. We soared over the flaming gate. When Bonny's front hooves hit the ground, I tumbled off of her. I lay in the dirt for a moment, gasping and coughing.

Timere stomped over and yanked me upward by the elbow. "Etta Alby—what in tarnation were you thinking? You could have died!"

"Timere—"

He pulled me close. I could hear his heart racing a million miles an hour—pounding faster than Bonny's hooves when she galloped flat out.

"I can't lose Bonny, Timere," I said, my words muffled by his shirt.

"I can't lose *you* Etta Alby." He kissed

the top of my head and rested his chin on it. "You're a fool."

"Yes, I know—and you can punish me for it later. But—" I struggled out of his grasp. "Timere, the fire…"

He pointed east. "It spread to the shack."

I gasped. "All our money—"

"I saved the saddlebags."

"What'll we do now?"

"We wait for the wind to die down. Then the fire will, as well."

I frowned. "Someone must have started the fire, Timere."

He swiped a hand through his hair, which he had recently cut so that it was shoulder-length again. "I know."

"Where are Bonny and Elm?"

"They'll come back—or someone will catch them."

The wind stopped, and gradually the fire died down. I stared at everything Timere and I had put together with our dreams and our own hands. The outhouse and corral were ashes. The shack was crumbling, but still standing.

My garden was dust. Wisps of smoke faded into the sky.

"Everything is gone," I said quietly. "Our home is destroyed."

"Maybe this is for the better," Timere said.

I gazed at him in shock. "What do you mean?"

"I've been keeping something from you."

"What is it?"

He sighed. "I've been setting aside money ever since I began earning it. I've always wanted to own a ranch. I figured you'd be angry if you found out—especially when we were in debt to Mrs. Lane."

"I'm not angry about that—but what are you saying?"

"I have enough to purchase a small piece of land. I want to leave Calico and start a ranch. Will you come with me?"

"Calico is my home now, Timere. There *is* much more of the world to see, but…" I considered his offer. "Every day has been a struggle to survive—but it's still my home. It's caused me to appreciate life—and the fact that I'm living and thriving."

"What are *you* saying?"

I clutched at my hair. "*I* don't even know. I want to go with you—but I feel as if I'd be leaving a piece of myself behind."

"Perhaps when you leave a piece of yourself behind and travel somewhere new, you discover a new piece of yourself. Isn't that what occurred when you escaped your Aunt Gertrude?"

"Yes…"

"So will you come? We can have horses, Etta. You can have as many horses as we can afford, and a pasture for Bonny to run in."

"I don't know, Timere. I have to dwell on it."

He stared at me a long moment. "Etta, if you come, will you marry me when we find a place of our own?"

My heart caught in my throat. "*Marry* you?"

"Will you?"

My heart boiled with feelings I didn't understand. "Timere, you can't bewilder me with all this information all at once. I need time to think."

His eyes shone with hurt, but all he said was, "Alright."

CHAPTER EIGHTEEN

M arshal Bismark caught Bonny and Elm for Timere and me. They were tied to stakes near the burned shack, and we slept outside in our newly purchased bedrolls. I spread mine on the other side of Bonny. Timere and I weren't speaking again. For the second time since I'd met him, our friendship was strange and unfamiliar. I turned my back to him, my mind rolling over his earlier words. Bonny's singed forelock tickled my cheek, and I reached up to rub her forehead.

Timere wanted me to *marry* him. He wanted us to *leave* Calico. I pondered this. What did Calico really hold for me? Was I chasing my dreams here? Was I living life the way I desired? And why did fear well in my chest at the thought of owning a ranch with Timere and marrying him?

I tossed and turned restlessly. Bonny nuzzled my face, and I found comfort smoothing her forelock and pressing my forehead to hers. The stars glittered in the sky.

The truth was, Calico wasn't beautiful, and it wasn't a wonderful place to live. It was dangerous and difficult and even more challenging than living with Aunt Gertrude. But the harsh environment had shaped *me*.

"But who is *me*?" I whispered into Bonny's mane, now standing beside her. "Who am *I*?"

I took a deep, shaky breath. "Timere?"

He was awake. "Yah."

"Bonny needs to stretch her legs. She can't sleep. Wanna get Elm and take a walk with us?"

"Sure."

We untied the horses and started leading them. It was quiet for a long time.

I finally broke the silence. "Timere, I have to be honest with you."

"No one's stopping you from doing *that*," he practically scoffed.

"I'm serious!"

"So am I."

I halted Bonny and faced him. We glowered at one another.

"I'm overwhelmed," I whispered. "There are so many miles ahead. I don't know who I want to be yet."

"You can be whoever you want to be," Timere's gaze softened, and he reached out to touch my cheek briefly.

"I want to go with you and own a ranch together."

"I'm glad."

I clenched my mother's necklace. "You asked me to marry you…I thought you loved Mary…"

"I love *you*, Etta Alby." Timere took my hands in his and kissed me gently.

I looked from him, to the sky, to the ground. "I love you in return, Timere—but I don't know who *me* is yet."

"That's what we'll find out."

"One thing still troubles me."

"What troubles you?"

I met his eyes. "Do you promise never to leave me, as my father did my mother? Do you promise never to cast me out? I promise never to hurt you, and I'll be loyal. Will you do the same?"

"I promise never to leave you—or cast you out," Timere murmured. "Will you marry me?"

"I will surely marry you."

Timere and I loaded Bonny and Elm with newly-bought supplies.

"Are you ready?" Timere asked me.

I nodded slowly and smiled. "I'm ready."

We mounted the horses and began trotting away from Calico. When we were quite a ways away from it I reined in Bonny. I glanced back at the mining town that had been my home for approximately two years.

Perhaps—many years from now—someone would walk through the town. Everyone would be gone, but would that person feel us? Would he hear the miners singing as they worked, the patient mules braying as they drew the carts, and the clink of silver that so many hoped for? Would he hear Lucy Lane greeting her customers, or spy Marshal Bismark tipping his hat to a lady? Would he feel the presence of Victoria Wordsworth as she politely demanded her way, or William Donovan boasting about Loot? Would the stranger walk down the dusty road, following ghostly laughter of the school-children at recess?

Perhaps if he strained to listen, the bellowing from the saloon would reach his ears. And if he trekked west of Maggie Mine he'd spy the outline of a stagecoach containing Mary Wickham hugging her grandmother. Perhaps he'd hear me singing to Bonny and Elm—hear Timere hammering at the corral fence. Would this stranger feel the ghosts of the past?

It didn't matter now. I had a new dream to chase. I thought I heard a whisper on the wind as I prepared to heel Bonny.

Fortune favors the brave and bold, Etta. Fate loves the fearless.

Bonny and I galloped to catch up with Timere and Elm. I tilted my head back to feel the wind on my face—let it billow my hair.

That same wind would follow me home.

EPILOGUE

Timere and I stood side by side, clutching
the reins of Bonny and Elm.

"What do you think of this place?" Timere
asked, following my gaze to the abandoned
California ranch in front of us.

We stood knee-deep in tall, brittle barley
weeds. There was a white house with a short
chimney, chipping paint, and a bushy tree
beside it. The barn close by was red and tilting
a little, but sturdy. A shed stood beside it, along
with an enormous pasture. The blue sky with a
few puffy white clouds stretched as far as the
eye could see.

"It's beautiful," I breathed. I loved the

forlorn, enchanting look about the place, as if it had been waiting for us all along.

We stripped the horses of the luggage and tack, trusting them to stay near. Bonny whinnied, her song ringing through the air. Elm imitated the sound, and she reared to remind him who was boss. The wind whipped her blond mane, and her hooves struck at sky. She and Elm galloped at full speed toward nothingness, then reeled and reared in unison, whinnying again—rejoicing in their freedom. They knew this was home.

Timere put an arm around me, and I leaned my head against his shoulder. This life journey had been hard, yes—but it mattered. God had been with us every step of the way. I'd learned to trust—to step outside of my comfort area and toward the unknown. What fun is life if you know every bend, every twist in the river of life, anyway? We were *made* to be courageous.

The barley weeds swayed in the wind as the horses danced and the sky stretched on.

We were home.